TWISTING PARALLELS

STEVE L CLARK

ORANGE OCTAVE PRESS

Twisting Parallels

Copyright © 2023 by Steve L Clark

All rights reserved.

No part of this publication may be reproduced, distributed, or transmitted in any form or by any means, including photocopying, recording, or other electronic or mechanical methods, without the prior written permission of the publisher, except as permitted by U.S. copyright law.

The story, all names, characters, and incidents portrayed in this production are fictitious. No identification with actual persons (living or deceased), places, buildings, and products is intended or should be inferred.

Cover art by Matt Wildasin

Stories edited by Brandon Applegate, Tasha Reynolds, and Don Tackett

OTHER WORKS BY STEVE L CLARK

Short Story Collections

The Collapse of Ordinary

Novellas

The Doors of Chamberlain

Down Home

CONTENTS

SHORT STORY LOVE

An Introduction

I love short stories. Film and television initially influenced my exposure to the format. It hearkens back to a youth filled with Goosebumps and Are You Afraid of the Dark, graduating to Tales From the Crypt, Tales from the Dark Side, and The Twilight Zone. Anthology films like Creepshow and more modern offerings like Trick R' Treat and the V/H/S series are all soft spots for me. As an avid reader, it was no surprise that short story collections would catch my eye, as well. Collections from Stephen King, Richard Matheson, and H. P. Lovecraft all shaped my perception of how stories can be told. EC Comics were the last piece of the puzzle. The gore-soaked pages of Tales From the Crypt, The Haunt of Fear, and the Vault of Horror hold a special place in my heart.

With my predisposed love of the format, I suppose it was only natural that my first completed works would be short stories. You can find those early works in my debut collection, The Collapse of Ordinary. After writing a couple novellas, it was only a matter of time before I returned with another collection. I think of short story collections like I do a new album of music. Whereas a novel or novella compares to a movie, a collection is like an album; it can have different tones, highs and lows, and different songs might connect with people in different ways. My favorite thing about the feedback I received from readers of The Collapse of Ordinary was hearing which story readers liked the most. To my delight, the answers were almost always different. One person's favorite story might not have even made the top five of someone else. I hope to see the same mixture of opinions this time around.

Whether you've read all my stuff or new to my work, I hope it leaves you entertained. There are short stories I've read that I will never forget. Stephen King's The Jaunt comes to mind. Perhaps there's a story in this book that you will never forget?

Let's find out.

BOBO'S WICKED CIRCUS

All three girls jumped when the bedroom door burst open and slammed into the wall. Kelly stood in the doorway with a crumpled sheet of paper in her outstretched hand and a devious smile on her face.

"Get a load of this," she said.

"Jesus," Michelle said, "you scared the hell out of us."

Janelle sat cross-legged on the floor by the door. She reached up and snatched the paper from Kelly's hand.

"The carnival?" Janelle asked. She frowned and ran a hand through her blonde hair, tucking it behind her ear. "That's what you're excited about? The carnival sucks."

"Ew, yeah," Tracey said. She sat across the room on an oversized bean bag chair. "It's the same thing every year. Crappy rides with creepy weirdos taking the tickets. No thanks."

"My dad won't even let me ride that stuff," Michelle said, as she went back to flipping through pages of a Tiger Beat magazine featuring a smiling Devin Sawa on the cover. "*No kid of mine is gonna ride something put together overnight by a bunch of vagrants.*"

The girls cracked up at the spot-on impression of Michelle's dad.

Kelly leaned over Janelle and planted a finger on the flier near the bottom. Janelle squinted at the page.

"Featuring the all new attraction Bobo's Wicked Circus." She looked up at Kelly.

"Bobo? What kinda name is that?" Tracey asked.

"A perfect name for a clown and a haunted circus attraction, and we are going." Kelly smiled as she crossed the room and plopped down on the bed next to Michelle.

"Are you serious?" Michelle rolled her eyes. "Sounds lame."

"I don't do clowns," Janelle said. "I watched that IT movie on TV, and it messed me up. I couldn't look at the sink drain for weeks."

"C'mon, what the hell else are we gonna do? School's been out for two weeks, and we haven't done anything cool." Kelly said.

Michelle sighed in defeat. "Fine, we'll go."

Kelly pumped her first in the air. "It's settled then," Kelly said. "The carnival opens Friday, and we will be there."

"If Michelle's dad will let her go," Janelle said.

"I'll probably have to get Kenny to go as a *chaperone*, but he'll be into it, anyway."

"Kenny can chaperone me," Janelle said.

"Gross," Michelle replied.

"Hey, it's not our fault your brother looks like Jonathan Taylor Thomas," Kelly said.

Michelle groaned. "I hope Bobo feeds you to a lion."

After a couple of hot, boring days, the opening night of the carnival arrived. Kelly showed up at Michelle's house to find Tracey and Janelle already there, waiting on the porch with Michelle.

"You bitches ready for Bobo?" Kelly called as she walked up the driveway?

"Shhh," Michelle hissed with alarm. "My parents are inside!"

Kelly rolled her eyes and started to fire back, but stopped when the screen door creaked open and Michelle's older brother, Kenny, stepped outside.

He was two years older than the girls, and fresh off his first year at the nearby community college. He was handsome with waves of dark brown hair hanging around a well-defined jaw-line and sparkling green eyes. He wore a cut-off t-shirt highlighting muscular tan arms, tattered cargo shorts, and sneakers. He smiled at the girls as the screen door rattled closed behind him.

"Hi, Kenny," Tracey said, flashing her best smile.

Kelly snickered, Janelle blushed, and Michelle rolled her eyes.

"What's up, ladies?"

"Ready to get this show on the road," Kelly said. "Janelle is so excited you could come with us."

Janelle's eyes widened in embarrassment, and she covered her flushed cheeks with her palms. "Oh my God," she mumbled through her fingers.

Kenny laughed. "Don't lie, Kelly. I know you begged Michelle to get me to go."

"I did not!" Kelly replied, hands on her hips.

"More like I begged Mom and Dad to let us go without you," Michelle said.

"Fat chance," Kenny said. He hopped down the two steps from the porch to the sidewalk and waved the girls after him. "No way they would let you go without a chaperone. Not a bunch of youths gone wild like you four."

"That's us," Kelly said. "Wild bitches."

"You wish," Tracey said. "She's all talk."

"We'll see about that when we're inside Bobo's Wicked Circus!" Kelly mocked a terrified face, then laughed with excitement. "I can't wait!"

"You're gonna be so disappointed," Michelle said. "Seriously, how good could it possibly be?"

"It doesn't have to be that great of a building as long as it's got scary clowns in it."

"God, I hate clowns," Janelle said.

"Don't worry about it," Kenny said. He reached out and wrapped his arm around Janelle. "I'll keep the clowns away."

Janelle's face turned an alarming shade of firehouse red.

"Aww," Kelly said and winked mischievously at her.

They reached Kenny's car at the end of the driveway. It was an old sedan with over two hundred thousand miles on it, passed down from his parents, but it still ran well, and he was proud of it. He pulled open the back door and stepped aside. "Ladies first."

Kelly pushed Tracey and Michelle forward and then cut off Janelle. "You can sit up front with Kenny."

"I hate you," Janelle whispered when Kenny had walked around the front of the car and was out of earshot.

"No, you don't. Quit being so damn shy and talk to him. I think he likes you," Kelly whispered back.

"Yeah, right."

"Stop dreaming and take a shot. You might be surprised."

Kenny had sat in the driver's seat and reached over to open the passenger door. It popped out and bumped Janelle's hip. "Oh, sorry, Janelle."

"You're fine," she said.

"You hear that Kenny? She thinks you're fine."

Janelle sat and closed the door, cheeks ablaze once again. "Shut up, Kelly."

Kenny laughed and fired up the engine. "Here we go, ladies. The carnival awaits!"

The carnival was on a large field behind the elementary school. In a couple months, it would serve as the athletic park for the local baseball, softball, and soccer teams. Now, in the warm sun of late June, it was filled with thrill rides, game tents, and food vendor trailers in wandering aisles. This year's carnival featured more attractions than in years past, and spilled past the school's property and into a stretch of vacant acreage owned by one of the local farmers, connected by a small wooden bridge across a narrow creek. Fortunately, it had been an unseasonably dry June, and the creek was barely a trickle of water slicing through rocks, mud, and debris.

Kenny pulled into the school parking lot and parked near the road. Though the carnival had only been open for less than an hour, the lot was already nearly full, and several clusters of people who lived in town were walking toward the field rather than fighting with traffic and trying to park.

"Looks like it's hopping already," Kenny said as he shut off the engine and hopped out.

The girls followed suit, and the group weaved their way through the cars toward the trail leading around the back of the school to the fields.

The sound of calliope music, shouts, and laughter drifted closer, accompanied by the smell of grilling food.

"First stop - lemon shake-up," Tracey said.

"If we're allowed," Michelle said. "Queen Kelly may not let us do anything until we've gone through the stupid haunted house."

"One, it's not a haunted house. It's a wicked circus. Way cooler than a haunted house. And, two, we're not doing Bobo's Wicked Circus in the daytime. We have to wait until it's dark."

"Come on," Janelle said. "I just want to get this over with."

"She's right, though," Kenny replied. "Haunted stuff is way scarier at night."

"I know. That's why I want to do it now."

Kenny wrapped his arm around her and squeezed her shoulder. "It'll be fine."

Janelle stiffened and turned to the other girls. Michelle rolled her eyes, but a trace of a smile teased the corners of her mouth. Tracey mocked surprise with comically wide eyes. Kelly winked and mouthed *"You're welcome"*.

Kenny sensed her embarrassment and let his arm fall away. "Well, we've got time to kill, so let's get some dinner and wristbands for the rides. That Chuck Wagon is calling my name. I can smell it from here. Then, we can see what rides they have this year. Other than Bobo's Circus, of course. That's the main attraction."

The group mingled through the rapidly thickening crowd of people and bought food from the various stands. Janelle and Tracey followed Kenny to the Chuck Wagon for burgers and fries. Kelly and Michelle grabbed slices of pizza from a stand called Marco's Eatery. All of them picked up lemon shake-ups. After they finished, they found the ticket booth near the front of the field. One by one, an orange bracelet was strapped on their wrists, granting them unlimited rides for the evening.

"Alright, ladies," Kenny said as they wandered away from the ticket booth. "Probably got two hours before it gets dark enough to venture into Bobo's domain."

"Don't wait too long," a voice said from behind them.

The group turned together, and Janelle shrieked.

A clown stood right behind them, smiling maniacally. His eyes were strained wide, and red blood vessels spider-webbed across the whites. A sloppy red oval was painted around his mouth, and his eye makeup was narrow and angled to give him a menacing look. He wore a typical baggy costume with oversized blue and yellow polka-dots scattered across it. Sprays of red paint intended to be blood spatter marked various spots.

"Bobo's Wicked Circus is an attraction you'll never forget. But, my little friends, it's a one-night only show."

"One-night only?" Kelly asked. "See, aren't you guys glad I made us come tonight?"

"Why only one night?" Tracey asked the clown. Her voice was steady, but a flicker of discomfort crossed her eyes. She didn't have a fear of clowns, but something about the man in sloppily applied grease paint bothered her.

"You'll have to come and find out for yourself." The clown's smile faded, drooping into a gaping oval revealing yellow-stained teeth made even more unsightly by the contrasting white face paint. A low chuckle emanated from him, and he turned and stalked away.

"Holy shit," Janelle whispered. "I'm not going through that thing."

"Oh, yes, you are." Kelly slapped her on the back, inciting a wince from Janelle. "We're all going together. You'll be fine, Janelle. I promise."

Janelle shook her head but didn't reply. She knew it was useless. Kelly always had to have her way. Arguing would get her nowhere, and she didn't want to make a scene and leave the carnival.

"Seriously, it'll be fine," Kenny said. His voice was soft and comforting, not at all like Kelly's insistent pushing. "I'll stay right by you. The trick is to try not to act scared. The actors in these places always focus on the people who seem the easiest to scare. If you're jumping at every sound, they'll be all over you. Just play it cool and stay with me."

Janelle nodded and smiled. "Alright. But, I still don't like it."

"Yes! Now let's go ride some shit and kill time until it gets dark." Kelly pumped her fists in the air, then hooked one arm through Michelle's and the other through Tracey's. "We're gonna go check out The Scrambler. Only three to a seat, though. Sorry, Janelle. I guess you'll have to ride with Kenny."

"Fine with me," Janelle said, suddenly embracing a level of confidence she hadn't shown before. Kenny's words of comfort had awakened a fire in her. She was done being the shy girl getting set up by her friends. Imitating Kelly, she hooked her arm through Kenny's. "In fact, we might do the scrambler later. Let's go see what else there is to do. Shall we?"

Kenny smiled at her. "We shall."

"Oooooh," Tracey said playfully.

"Get it, girl," Kelly said.

Michelle shook her head and smiled. It was nice to see Janelle make a move. She was a nice girl. For all the crap she gave her brother, Kenny was a good guy, and she liked the idea of him and Janelle being a thing. "Take care of her, Kenny. Keep the clowns away."

"Absolutely," he said. He gave a salute to his sister, then pulled Janelle with him and away from the group.

Janelle fell into step beside him and let herself relax. Nervous excitement buzzed through her body like a low voltage current of electricity in her veins. Her self-doubt would never have imagined she'd be walking through the carnival midway arm-in-arm with Kenny, but here she was. She caught glances from other girls from school, noticing and whispering to their friends. For once, the attention did not embarrass her. Kenny's confidence oozed into her, and she held her head high.

"I don't know about you," Kenny said, "but I'm thinking about the Ferris wheel. You game?"

Janelle looked up at the giant wheel rotating slowly into the sky. "Let's do it."

He smiled and led her down the midway toward the wheel.

Neither of them saw the clown leaning against one of the nearby sideshow game booths, watching them go.

"I told you he was into her." Kelly sat smashed in between Tracey and Michelle in the scrambler cart, waiting for the ride to start. A grungy middle-aged man walked from cart to cart, checking the latches and dropping the metal pins into the locks.

"I never said he wasn't," Michelle said. "I just didn't think she would ever get the guts to make a move. He wasn't going to push himself on a girl who didn't show any interest. He's not that kind of guy."

The ride attendant finished checking the carts and positioned himself on a stool behind the operator controls. He gave the carts a final sweep with bored, droopy eyes, then pressed a button on the console. The hydraulics came to life with an audible hum and metal squeaked as each section of carts began to spin.

With each spin of the cart, the girls slid toward the outer edge, smashing Tracey into the wall. As the ride picked up speed and the arms turned faster, the cart whipped sharply toward the metal fence barricading the ride before rocketing back across to the opposite side. The girls laughed and shouted, hair slapping wildly in the steady bursts of wind produced by the speeding cart.

Michelle was the first to notice the clown. Each time the cart reached the outer edge, the riders were only a couple feet from bystanders waiting along the fence, brought nearly face-to-face for a split second before spinning away and hurtling to the other side. Michelle had been watching Tracey groan in comical discomfort every time the momentum pressed them into her, but as the ride swung them toward the fence near the operator station, she saw him. It was the same clown who had approached them on the midway. He stared at the ride with no trace of amusement on his face.

Michelle stopped laughing and twisted her neck to keep him in her sight. After a moment, she knew one thing for sure. The clown wasn't watching the ride. He was watching *them*. His cold stare never left their cart.

"Guys," she called, but her voice was carried away by the rushing wind. When neither girl acknowledged her, she jabbed an elbow into Kelly's ribs.

"Ow. What the hell?"

"Look," Michelle said, leaning close so that her lips were by Kelly's ear. "That clown is staring at us."

Kelly twisted, and her eyes fell on the clown. He hadn't moved and his expression had not changed. The cart twisted again, this time delivering them directly in front of the clown.

"Bobo!" Kelly shouted. She raised her hand and blew him a kiss just as the cart twisted them away.

"Ew, stop it," Tracey said. Her forehead scrunched up in disgust. "That guy is gross."

"I don't like it," Michelle said. "It's creepy."

"Uh, yeah. That's kind of the point. Scary clown? He's supposed to be creepy," Kelly said.

The droning sound of hydraulics shifted downward, and the carts slowed. When the ride came to a complete stop, their cart was on the opposite side, facing away from the operator and the clown. Kelly reached out and pulled the metal pin free, then shoved the gate open.

"Let's go talk to him," Kelly said. She climbed over Tracey's legs and hopped out of the cart first. "Come on!"

"I don't want to," Michelle said.

"Me neither. Dude is weird."

"Ugh, you guys are lame." Kelly stepped aside so the girls could climb out. "He's gone, anyway."

Michelle exited last and turned to look. The grungy ride operator still sat on his stool watching the riders exit the area, but the clown had gone. She looked around the midway, expecting to find him by the exit gate waiting for them, but there was no clown in sight.

"Good," Tracey said. "I don't want to sound like Janelle, but I'm kind of not feeling this haunted circus thing."

Michelle nodded agreement, but Kelly would have none of it. "Stop being babies," she said, making no effort to hide the annoyance in her voice. "I had no idea you were all such chickens." She led them through the swinging exit gate and back onto the midway. "Let's go see if we can find Janelle and Kenny. Probably riding the Tunnel of Love." She cackled and marched away, and the girls followed.

In the sky, the sun inched closer to the horizon. Darkness would fall soon.

"There they are," Tracey said, and pointed.

The girls had wandered the carnival for a good twenty minutes before they found them. Dusk had fallen and the carnival field glowed with colorful lights flickering and flashing from one end to the other.

Janelle and Kenny stood together a few game booths down the midway from where the girls had stopped to scan the crowd. They talked animatedly, paying no attention to the carnival patrons around them. Janelle held a wand of blue cotton candy in one hand, and her other arm was wrapped around a large teddy bear, clutching it to her side.

"Oh my God," Kelly squealed as the girls approached the couple. "You guys are adorable!"

Janelle blushed. "He won me a teddy bear." She nodded toward the game booth next to them. Several plywood cutouts painted to look like football players lined the back of the booth. Each figure had a tire inserted into a circular opening cut into the chest, and players got three tries at throwing a football through the holes.

"Got all three of them," Kenny said. He smiled and did the classic Heisman trophy pose.

"You're a dork," Michelle said. "Are you buying cotton candy for all of us or just your *friend?*"

"I didn't buy it," Kenny replied, then leaned toward Janelle and took a big bite off the top. "She did, and we're sharing. Buy your own."

"I don't want cotton candy," Kelly said. "I want to go to the circus!"

Tracey frowned. "I'm team Janelle, now. I don't want to do it any-more." She recounted the events on the Scrambler to Kenny and Janelle. "That guy is weird."

Kelly rolled her eyes. "I told you guys, he's supposed to be weird. This isn't a kiddie ride. It's supposed to be scary, so he's being scary."

"It didn't feel like he was acting for the show," Michelle said. "It felt weird. Like, not safe."

"You guys are ridiculous. Fine, I'll go through it by myself. I think there's a merry-go-round up by the front. That sounds like it might be more your speed," Kelly said. She turned from the group and stormed down the midway.

The group watched her go for a moment, then turned to each other.

"What do you girls think? You want to let her go by herself? I'm fine either way," Kenny said.

"I really don't want to go," Michelle said. "I've got bad vibes from that weird clown. But that makes me not want her to go by herself either. If he is a weirdo and tries to do something creepy, she won't have anyone there to help her."

"I was thinking the same thing," Tracey mumbled. "We can't let her go by herself. Let's just go with her and get it over with. It's probably fine, but just in case, I'd rather we be together. The guy's not going to try anything with a whole group of us, right?"

"It'll be fine," Kenny said. "The guy is just doing his job, and doing it very well, it seems. He's definitely gotten under your skin."

"Come on," Janelle said. "Let's catch up before she goes in."

With all in agreement, they made their way through the crowd, which had grown exponentially since they had arrived. The midway was nearly shoulder to shoulder, with patrons traveling up and down the paths.

"I think we need to go that way," Kenny shouted. A nearby attraction blared pop music and his voice died in the mix.

"What?" Janelle called back.

"That way!" Kenny pointed toward the back end of the field.

"Yeah, we saw it earlier," Tracey shouted.

They pushed through the rest of the midway section of the carnival. The crowd thinned out slightly as they reached the rear of the field, which was primarily sectioned off for the bigger rides.

"I don't see her," Michelle said. There was a note of concern in her voice.

"I don't either," Tracey replied. "We have to go faster."

They nodded and increased their pace. In the distance, they could make out the fiery red glow of fluorescent letters.

Bobo's Wicked Circus

Kelly approached the attraction with mixed emotions. She was annoyed with her friends for chickening out, but was still excited to go through. Bobo's Wicked Circus was set up on a long trailer. It impressed Kelly that such a realistic-looking building could be on a mobile trailer bed. It was two stories tall and completely enclosed. The exterior had several evil clowns painted in bright colors, all taking part in various circus activities. One stood laughing next to a lion with a blood soaked severed arm hanging from its mouth. Another was diving through a flaming ring. Its hair had caught fire, and it smiled maniacally. It was cartoonish, but effective. Circus music piped from two large speakers mounted in the upper corners of the building.

Only one group was in the line, three younger boys, and they slipped inside as she approached. She turned and looked behind her, hoping to see her friends had come along after her, but there was no sign of them. She rolled her eyes and huffed.

"Well, well, well," said a gravelly voice.

Kelly recognized it at once. She spun back and saw Bobo had emerged from the entrance. He smiled wickedly.

"What happened to your friends?"

"They're pussies," Kelly said.

Bobo chuckled. "Surely you aren't thinking about going through my wicked circus alone, are you? That wouldn't be wise. No, not at all."

"I'm a big girl."

"I see that," Bobo said. His gaze slid deliberately down her body and back up. "All grown up, you are."

Kelly cringed, and for the first time, she felt a tinge of fear. She had dismissed her friends' opinions about the clown being a creep, convinced he was just playing the role. Now, she wasn't sure, and she felt vulnerable. Maybe going in alone wasn't a good idea.

Bobo seemed to sense her hesitation and sneered. "Not as brave as you thought, eh?"

Anger flared in her eyes, and she stomped forward. "I'm not scared of you, or your stupid circus." She stopped inches from the clown. A wave of sweat and grime wafted off him, turning her stomach, but she clenched her jaw and held his gaze.

"In that case, welcome to the show," Bobo said. He grinned and stepped aside with a showman's wave, leading her to the entrance. "I hope you make it out in one piece, my dear."

Kelly rolled her eyes and walked up the short staircase, then stepped into the darkened hallway leading inside. Behind her, she heard Bobo chuckling again.

"Shit, there she goes!"

The group turned to Michelle, who pointed at the attraction.

"That was her. She just went inside," Michelle groaned.

"Okay," Kenny said. "Let's go catch up with her. She's not that far ahead. And look, there's Bobo outside."

The girls looked and saw the clown watching the entrance doorway. As if he could feel their eyes on him, he whipped back toward them. He studied them for a moment, then a mischievous grin stretched the smeared red oval of his mouth. He turned and ran inside.

"Jesus," Kenny moaned. "Come on. This guy has it out for us tonight. He's probably going to harass Kelly all the way through it."

They jogged over to the trailer and filed into the entrance. Kenny took the lead, with Janelle holding his hand and sticking close. Michelle followed behind Janelle, and Tracey brought up the rear. The entrance walkway turned to the left and opened into a narrow room featuring a lifted platform with metal railings. A giant wheel painted in black and white spirals rotated around the platform, creating a disorienting effect. Strobe lights flashed, increasing the dizzying effect. Kenny stepped onto the platform, then tilted sideways and bumped into the railing. All four of them clutched the railing and staggered their way across the platform.

"I think I'm gonna puke," Tracey groaned from behind them.

"Close your eyes," Michelle said. "Hold on to the rail and close your eyes. It'll be easier."

Tracey followed her instructions and felt her way to the end of the platform. She opened her eyes and stepped down with the rest of the group. A thick black curtain hung over the entrance to the next room, and Kenny pushed it aside.

More strobe lights battered their senses as they stepped through the curtain. A voiceover of a circus showman piped through speakers somewhere above them. He shouted in a panicked voice with a mixture of audience screams and savage roars.

The lion is loose in the stands! Save yourselves!

The room was decorated to be a small oval-shaped theater with bleacher seating wrapped around it. Mannequins and stuffed prop bodies were scattered all over the seats in various states of carnage. Blood-covered severed limbs and ravaged bodies were staged on the ground and hanging over the barrier wall separating the stands from the floor. A section of the wall had collapsed, allowing them to walk through the showcase and into a door on the other side.

"This is disgusting," Janelle said.

Kenny nodded and squeezed her hand. "Just keep moving. Don't look at it."

"For a shitty carnival thing, these effects look really good," Michelle said.

"I know," Tracey replied. She looked around nervously as she walked through. Her foot came down on a slick tube painted to look like a strand of intestines and she nearly fell. Her stomach lurched, and she swallowed hard, fighting against the nausea stirring in her stomach. The tendril squished under her foot and a glob of red and yellow goo oozed out of it. She gagged and turned away. *What the hell is that made of?*

She turned back and panicked when she saw the rest of the group passing through the next curtain. Kenny and Janelle were already through, and Michelle held the curtain back. Michelle looked back and waved her on.

"I'm coming." She jogged the rest of the way through the show floor and grabbed the curtain. Michelle vanished into the pitch dark hall beyond. Tracey took one step inside, then paused. A movement in her peripheral vision caught her eye. She turned and let out a split second of a scream before the clown was on her. He clamped his hand over her mouth, then wrapped his arm around her in a tight hug, pinning her arms to her side. She bucked and kicked, but his grip did not loosen. He dragged her away from the curtain and into a doorway concealed near the entrance on the other side. The clown chuckled as she fought to break free.

"You're a feisty one! Good! The lion likes to hunt. It's more fun when his food fights back!"

The hidden door opened, and the clown shoved her into another darkened room. She twisted and fell, landing softly on a pile of straw. The clown chuckled once more, then slammed the door closed, eliminating the flashing strobes from the stadium room. Tracey screamed, then scrambled to her feet. The air smelled musty and thick. It reminded her of the zoo. It was a primal, animal smell. She put her hands out in front of her and walked slowly until she felt the wall. Then she inched her way back toward where she thought the door was located. She took slow, shuffling steps, trying not to risk falling down. The straw scratched her ankles and calves. She had taken three steps when a sound stopped her.

Somewhere behind her, a deep growl rumbled. Her blood froze and her eyes bulged. This wasn't possible. It couldn't be real. Her mind flashed back to the carnage in the stadium room. She thought of how realistic the bodies had looked. The growl came again, this time closer. Her entire body quivered, and she sank into a ball.

"Please, no," she whispered through tears.

There was a final snarl, then the sound of heavy steps rushing toward her. She covered her head with her arms and closed her eyes. Then she screamed as claws, fangs, and fur smothered her. The last thing she heard, mixed with the hungry snarls of the beast, was the sound of the circus showman echoing through the speakers in the next room.

The lion is loose in the stands! Save yourselves!

Kenny tightened his grip on Janelle's hand and led them into the next room. A short hall with another black curtain at the end cloaked them in darkness. When he pulled back the next curtain, they found themselves in a room dimly lit by a single red bulb on the ceiling in the center. Kenny jolted to a stop.

The room was packed full with clowns.

Janelle sucked in a startled breath and pressed herself against Kenny.

"Jesus," Michelle whispered.

"They're just dummies," Kenny said. He reached for the nearest clown and flicked it in the forehead. A hollow tap echoed from within. "See?"

"I know. I just hate clowns," Janelle said.

"Let's just get through this. Kelly can't be that far ahead of us. And this place can't be that big. She might even be waiting outside." Kenny pointed across the room. "The exit is over there. Let's go."

He took a couple steps, Janelle shuffling right beside him, then Michelle called out.

"Wait, where's Tracey?"

Kenny and Janelle turned back and confirmed Tracey wasn't with Michelle.

"She was right behind me." Frustrated, Michelle stomped back to the curtain and yanked it aside. "Come on, Tracey! I want to get out of here."

There was no response from the darkened hallway. She could still hear the announcer from the stadium room, but Tracey did not answer her call.

"Maybe she turned back?" Janelle asked.

Michelle chewed her lip. "I don't know. I mean, she was pretty freaked out by all the blood and guts in that last room, but wouldn't she have said something if she was going back?"

"She could have panicked," Kenny said. He let go of Janelle's hand and walked quickly back through the hallway. He pulled back the curtain leading to the stadium room, looked inside, then returned to the girls. "She's not in there. She had to have gone back."

"That doesn't seem like her," Janelle said.

"What else could it be? That clown guy freaked her out earlier, and she already didn't want to go through this. Maybe that room was the last straw, and she bailed in a hurry? Let's just keep moving. I'm over this." Kenny grabbed Janelle's hand again and waved at Michelle. "Let's go."

Michelle frowned, uncertain that Tracey would take off like that, but what other option did they have? Reluctantly, she let the curtain go and followed Kenny and Janelle into the sea of clowns.

Each clown was dressed and painted to look different. Some of them were the standard fare and made up to look like normal circus clowns with cheery smiles. Others had menacing expressions painted on their faces and wore blood soaked costumes like the one Bobo had worn out on the midway. The floor was designed to give under their weight as they walked causing the mannequins to sway and move as they passed. It was an unsettling effect, and Michelle quickened her pace, bumping into Janelle. Janelle squealed in alarm and twisted around.

"Don't do that," she hissed.

"I'm sorry. Go faster. I want out of here."

"So do I," Janelle fired back.

"Come on, girls. We're almost there," Kenny said, trying to calm them down. "We're all a little freaked out. Let's not fight with each other."

They weaved through the last section of clowns and reached a bright red door. Kenny twisted the knob and pulled it open. He turned and gently pulled Janelle into the doorway. At the end of the hall was another door with a fluorescent EXIT sign hanging above it. He turned to Michelle.

"See, there's the exit. Nothing to worry..." His voice trailed off and his eyes widened in surprise.

The clown next to Michelle sprang to life. It drew back a hand wielding a large serrated knife with blue and yellow polka dots painted on the handle and slashed the blade across Michelle's throat.

Michelle's mouth gaped, and a wheezing sound hissed through her lips. She grabbed at her neck as blood streamed down her chest. Her mouth quivered, and she collapsed to her knees.

The clown turned to Kenny and Janelle with a wide smile. "Surprise! The circus always has surprises!"

Kenny was frozen, his face a mask of horror and surprise. He stared dumbfounded as his sister collapsed face first onto the floor. Janelle let out a blood-curdling scream, waking him from his stupor. Without thinking, he dashed forward and delivered a kick to the clown's chest.

The clown flew backwards, knocking over a pile of mannequin clowns and groaned in pain.

"Run!" Kenny screamed at Janelle, and pulled her after him, through the doorway and down the last hall. The EXIT sign lit their way as they raced to the door.

"Always a surprise at the circus!" The clown called after them. He chuckled, then groaned in pain. "Save the best for last!"

They reached the end of the hall, and Kenny's fist wrapped around the doorknob. With a violent yank, he threw the door open, then froze. Instead of seeing the sky and the lights of the carnival midway, they were in another dimly lit room. A single figure stood inside.

"Kelly?" Janelle asked. She rushed forward and grabbed her friend by the shoulder.

Kelly wore a baggy clown costume and her face had been covered in grease paint. Her mouth was painted in a deep frown, making her look comically sad. She swayed and looked up at Janelle. Her eyes were glazed, and her pupils were dilated.

"Bee-boo," Kelly said. Her voice was heavy and slurred.

Kenny leaned in front of her and studied her face. "Kelly, what happened to you? Did that asshole drug you?"

"Bee-boo," she said again.

Janelle sobbed. "What are you saying? What's Bee Boo? We have to get out of here!"

"Bee-boo. My...name is...Bee-boo...the clown."

A chorus of laughter erupted from behind them and they spun around. Bobo stood inside the doorway, still clutching a hand against his chest. Four more clowns stood flanking him, two on each side, all holding weapons. Two held knives, one gripped a taser that crackled and sparked, and the last held an oversized mallet.

Kenny pushed Janelle behind him with one arm and stood between the girls and the clowns. With increasing horror he realized the others must have been hiding in the clown room all along.

"I'm sorry to say that Bobo's Wicked Circus is now closed for the night. We must be on our way! Our stay in your little town was delightful. We've even added one to our ranks. I'm pleased to announce the newest member of Bobo's Wicked Circus, Bee-Boo the Clown!"

The other clowns cheered, and Bobo bowed. Then he turned to Kenny and sneered. "I'm afraid there's only room for one more. You two will have to go, and we certainly can't have you telling all our surprises. No, sir! We have so many more towns to visit and entertain! We thank you for coming. We hope you've enjoyed the show. But, alas, it's time to turn down the lights. Rippy-Roo, if you please!"

One of the other clowns pranced over to the wall and flipped open a breaker box. With a cackle, he flipped a switch and the dim light plunged them into darkness.

Kenny tensed and readied himself to fight. Behind him, Janelle screamed. There was a loud click and suddenly the room flashed in pulses from a strobe light. Kenny squinted through watery eyes and shouted in despair as the clowns closed in. He threw a punch at the first, knocking them away, but he could not turn fast enough. The oversized mallet smashed into the back of his head and he collapsed. Janelle's screams washed over him as his life faded. His eyes found Kelly, still standing where she had been, watching in dazed indifference. Her mouth moved, and Kenny strained to hear her over the screams and laughs assaulting him. As he slipped from consciousness and into death, her words came clear.

"Bee-Boo. My name is Bee-Boo the clown."

37 ROOMS

alcolm Friedkin opened his eyes. At first, he saw only blurs of beige and white. He blinked twice and his vision cleared slightly, revealing a beige wall adorned with a whiteboard. He squinted through the haze and made out words written on the board.

Date: May 15

Your nurse Is: Elaine

Your doctor Is: Dr. Leonard

As awareness settled in, he noticed a consistent beeping sound from behind. He turned to look and grimaced. Pain rippled through his body, and his head felt like an anvil pressing into his shoulders. He looked down with his eyes only, careful to keep his throbbing head still, and saw the rest of his body. A white blanket was pulled up to his chest, but his arms were exposed. Deep bruising splashed across them both. An IV ran from his arm and snaked off the bed and out of sight.

Hospital. I'm in a hospital.

He groaned. The more his mind cleared, the more he noticed the pain radiating throughout his entire body. *What the hell happened?*

As if on cue, a door opened, hinges creaking a protest that echoed off the walls. Malcolm shot his eyes to the left and saw a nurse. She wore a face mask, but he could tell from her eyes she was young. He tried to speak, but his throat allowed only another groaning croak.

"Well, hello there, Mr. Friedkin. You've finally joined us." Her name badge twirled on a cord around her neck, but held steady long enough for him to see she was indeed the Elaine the whiteboard had promised. She swiped a thermometer across his forehead, then typed the results into the computer on the stand by his bed. "Fever's down, too. That's excellent! You were worrying us."

Malcolm cleared his throat, wincing at the dryness. "What happened?" he asked, his voice barely a whisper.

She strapped a blood pressure cuff onto his arm. It hummed to life and constricted. He scrunched his face as the pressure built until he was sure the thing had malfunctioned, and his arm would simply fall off. A panicked cry filled his chest, but the motor stopped and the cuff hissed, releasing the pressure.

"Hmm, your blood pressure is still a little high, but nothing too crazy."

"What happened?" he asked again. This time his voice came louder, though still cracked and hoarse.

"You were in an accident, Mr. Friedkin."

"What kind of accident?"

"Car accident," she said. She walked around to the other side of the bed and checked the fluid bags hanging from the metal IV pole.

Malcolm searched his mind to remember a car accident, but his memory was blank. He was distraught to realize he couldn't remember much of anything. He knew his name, but that was about it.

"I don't remember."

"Hmm, yes. We thought that might happen. You were unresponsive at the scene, and we've had you in a medically induced coma since you arrived. It will take some time for your memories of the accident to come back. Trauma like that can cause cognitive issues with the brain."

"How long?"

"I couldn't say. Some people get it back fairly quickly, others take a—"

"No. How long have I been here?"

"Oh, I'm sorry. About a week and a half now." She returned to the computer and scrolled through the screen. "Yeah, eleven days today."

Eleven days?

"The doctor will want to talk to you as soon as he comes in for his rounds tomorrow morning. Is there anyone you want us to call? We've been unable to find any family or friends to contact about your condition."

Malcolm tried to think, but his mind was hopelessly blank. "I don't know. I can't remember."

"It's okay, Mr. Friedkin," Elaine said. She stepped to the side of the bed and patted his arm. "Don't upset yourself. Hopefully, you'll start remembering things sooner rather than later. How's your pain?"

Malcolm groaned in response.

"Pretty bad, huh? I'll put in an order for another dose of morphine. That should help take the edge off and let you rest. Try to relax, and I'll be back shortly."

She typed a note into the computer, the clacking keys acting as tiny volts of agony prodding his aching head, then walked swiftly out of the room. He closed his eyes and fought against the nausea building in his stomach. It reminded him of the few times he'd had migraines. He always got sick and threw up when he had migraines.

Hey, I remembered something, he thought. *I get migraines. My name is Malcolm and sometimes I get migraines.*

Time passed, though he lacked the awareness to put any measure to it, and Elaine returned.

"I've got your meds, Mr. Friedkin," she said, injecting the clear liquid into his IV. "This should help you rest. Can I get you anything?"

He stared up at her. He felt like he *should* need something, but he didn't know what. After a moment, he shook his head gingerly.

"If you think of anything, press the call button on your remote." She lifted the bulky plastic television remote and pointed to the big red button at the base. "That'll call the nurses' station." She put the remote near his hand and left the room.

Alone again, he turned his head to the side and looked out the window. The sky was dark and there was nothing visible to show where he might be. A red brick wall blocked any view of the surrounding landscape. The structure filled most of his view, and he decided he must be in a fairly large hospital.

But where? He closed his eyes and tried to dive deep into his memory banks. *I don't even know what city or state this is. I don't know where I live.* The sheer blankness of his memory taunted him, and a new feeling emerged.

Fear.

He was alone, with no memory and no one to tell him anything. Suddenly, a voice spoke in his head, further driving home his isolation. *No one is here to tell you anything because you have no one. It's been eleven days. That's what she said, right? They haven't been able to find anyone to contact in eleven days. Don't you think someone would be looking for you by now? Of course they would. But they haven't, and you know what that means. You are alone.*

A single tear slipped over the rim of his eye and coursed through the stubble on his cheek. Emotions swelled in his chest, but he fought against them. His body ached profusely, and the wracking sobs pushing to be unleashed would be torturous. Instead, he locked his jaw and focused on the wall across from the bed. To the right of the white board hung a painting of a sloping grassy field under a blue sky punctuated by blips of white clouds. It reminded him of the intro to Little House on the Prairie. He half expected to see a young girl come skipping through the tall grass. *Little House on the Prairie,* he thought. *I used to watch that when I was a kid. I used to watch it with...*

He couldn't remember.

As he stared at the painting, he noticed a change in his condition. Subtle at first, a stream of relief seemed to travel through his veins. The deep ache in his body lessened and his mind fogged over. Morphine. Nurse Elaine had given him morphine, and it was hitting his system. His eyelids grew heavy and a moment later he was asleep again.

When he woke, a man sat in the chair across the room. He wore a dark suit over a red silk dress shirt. His leg was crossed over his knee, and Malcolm could see the fluorescent lights reflecting brightly off his shiny black dress shoes. The man was clean shaven and neatly groomed. His hair was as black as his suit and slicked over to one side. He smiled politely.

"Welcome back, Mr. Friedkin."

Malcolm cleared his throat and shifted on the bed. A mild jolt of discomfort hit, but he was relieved to find it wasn't as intense as the last time he'd tried to move.

"How are you feeling?"

"I'm okay, I suppose," Malcolm said. "All things considered."

The man smiled, and his eyebrow twitched upward. "All things considered, indeed."

"Are you the doctor? I'm sorry if we've already met. I don't remember."

"I am a doctor. We've met before, but that's okay if you don't remember."

"I apologize. What is your name?"

"No need for apologies. I'm Saxan."

"Dr. Saxan?"

"Yes," the man said, "that's right. Dr. Saxan."

Saxan. That name didn't ring any bells. Had Elaine told him the doctor's name? He didn't think she had.

"How are things looking?" Malcolm noticed his voice sounded stronger. He was still hoarse, but the weak quivering had lessened.

"Very well, Mr. Friedkin. You are improving as expected."

Malcolm nodded. "I feel better. Not great, but definitely better than yesterday. Or earlier. I don't know when that was, actually."

Dr. Saxan laughed. "Ah, time is like that, isn't it? So fleeting, so unpredictable."

Malcolm studied the doctor. "I never thought of it that way, but I suppose it is."

The doctor's face grew serious. "It is indeed. Make no mistake. I've considered it at great length."

An awkward silence passed between them. Malcolm shifted. He wasn't sure how to respond, so he changed the subject back to his care. "So, how much longer do you think I'm going to be in here?"

"Well, that depends. If your physical recovery continues on its current trajectory, I imagine I might release you within the next week. I say potentially, because your physical recovery may play second fiddle to your mental recovery. We can't exactly let you go with no memory. Where would you go?"

Malcolm considered, and his brow bunched up in frustration. Then he let out a defeated sigh. "That's a good point. I still don't really remember anything."

"Yes. That is unfortunate, but the hope is it will be temporary. Scans of your brain show no visible damage other than the swelling you had when you came in. That has gone down, so there's no physical reason your memory shouldn't return to full capacity in time. The big question is, how much time?"

"Is there anything I can do to help the process?"

The doctor stood and strolled casually around the side of the bed until he stood above Malcolm. His face was friendly enough, but his eyes were hard. Malcolm picked up the scent of a peculiar cologne drifting from him.

"May I ask you a question, Mr. Friedkin?"

Malcolm nodded.

"Do you *want* to remember?"

Malcolm stared up at the doctor. Confusion blossomed on his face. "Of course I want to remember. Why would you ask that?"

"Are you sure about that?"

"Yes," Malcolm said. His voice was stern, showcasing his frustration. "I don't understand why you would ask me that."

"I just wonder if perhaps your amnesia is driven by an intentional effort to forget. Perhaps what you've done is so terrible you are trying to block it from your mind, and in doing so, you've blocked nearly everything from your mind."

"What do you mean, 'what I've done'?"

The doctor smiled and walked back around the bed, approaching the IV pole beside it. "Now, now, Mr. Friedkin. It will do your recovery no good at all to get excited." He pressed a button on the stand, then pressed it again. The machine beeped twice.

Instantly, Malcolm felt a surge through his veins. His eyelids fluttered as he fought the wave of sleep crashing in on him. "Why did you do that?"

"Rest, Mr. Friedkin. Sleep is the best medicine. We will chat again when you've had time to rest and calm yourself."

"I am ... calm," Malcolm said, the last word slurring into something that sounded more like "cahhhhh" than "calm". He tried to watch the doctor as he walked away, but his vision blurred and the last image he registered before drug induced sleep took him was a smear of black and red at the foot of his bed.

Malcolm woke to find the room empty. He was groggy. Trying to focus took extreme effort. A bitter, copper taste filled his mouth, and his lips were parched. He turned his head and spotted a plastic water cup with a straw sticking out on the tray stand near the bed. Malcolm lifted his arm and reached for the edge of the stand. He was amazed by how weak he was. His arm felt like it weighed a hundred pounds, and his hand trembled against the urge to drop back on to the bed.

His fingers reached the bottom lip of the tray, and he tugged it toward him. The wheels squeaked as it rolled forward. He gripped the green handle of the cup and brought the straw to his lips, being careful not to drop it. The first sip hit his mouth, and he moaned with delight. No drink of water had ever been more welcomed in his life.

"Yes, cold water is perhaps the greatest medicine of all."

Malcolm lurched in surprise and the water shot into his nose. The cup clattered to the floor. He launched into a coughing fit, flinching in agony as the deep coughs wracked his body. His eyes darted to the corner of the room and landed on Dr. Saxan.

The doctor watched Malcolm coughing and choking with an amused grin on his face. "Although, as you've learned, in your condition, it is best to go slow."

"When did you get here?" Malcolm asked after the coughing fit expired.

"I've been here the whole time, Mr. Friedkin."

"You weren't here a minute ago when I woke up."

"Wasn't I?" Dr. Saxan cocked his head and stared patiently at Malcolm.

Malcolm considered. He had been extremely fog-headed when he woke. No doubt a side effect from the double shot of morphine the doctor had sent through his IV. He supposed it was possible he hadn't noticed the doctor on the other side of the room. The water cup had distracted him, after all. Still, he was unsettled.

"I sure didn't see you, but I suppose you must have been. You certainly didn't come in through the door while I was drinking."

"No, I certainly did not."

Their previous conversation returned to Malcolm's mind. "Why did you knock me out like that? And why did you ask if I was forgetting on purpose?"

"Very good," the doctor said. "I was afraid you might not remember our last conversation."

"Oh, I remember. Truth be told, I don't like your suggestion. I may not remember much, but I don't believe I'm a bad person. Whatever it is you think I might have done, you're wrong."

"Am I?" Dr. Saxan crossed the small room and stood next to the bed. His fingers coiled around the handrail, and Malcolm noticed the man's fingernails were long and glassy.

"Yes," Malcolm said, though his voice trembled slightly, "you are." He found himself uncomfortable and intimidated by the doctor. He took a deep breath and pushed on. "In fact, I think I would like a second opinion on my treatment. Nothing personal, but I'm not comfortable with your diagnosis."

Dr. Saxan chuckled. "Have I offended you?"

"You have."

"How dreadfully inconsiderate of me. I'm afraid my bedside manner is not my strongest suit. Do you insist on seeing another doctor?"

Malcolm stared at the doctor. Something in the man's eyes frightened him, but he maintained contact and gave a single nod.

"Very well. I will notify the nurse," Dr. Saxan said. He turned and sauntered to the end of the bed.

Malcolm sighed in relief. He hadn't expected the doctor to accept his request so easily.

"Mr. Friedkin," the doctor said, his back still turned.

"Yes?"

"I suspect as your memories return, a number will come to the forefront of your mind. That number is 37. It's a dreadful number, and one you should be ashamed of, but you are not."

Malcolm watched the doctor approach the white board and lift the dry-erase marker from the tray. He removed the cap and drew the number thirty-seven at the top right corner, just above where Elaine had written her name.

"Thirty-seven is the number you want to forget, but I won't let you." Dr. Saxan turned and sneered at Malcolm. "You will remember, and you will pay." He put his foot on the padded chair in the corner of the room and stepped up onto it. He flashed Malcolm a hateful gaze, then lifted his left leg into the air.

Malcolm stared in dazed confusion as the doctor kicked the painting on the wall. When the thud he expected to hear did not come, his mouth dropped in horrified disbelief. The doctor's leg sank into the painting, merging with faded colors. He leaned forward and pushed his head and chest through, barely clearing to the top of the frame. His right leg slithered through, and then he was gone. A water-colored version of Dr. Saxan now stood in the field, staring through the frame with hate in his eyes.

Malcolm screamed.

"I know this must be difficult for you to process, but I assure you, Mr. Friedkin, there is no Dr. Saxan on this staff. My name is Dr. Leonard, and you've been under my care since you arrived here."

Malcolm did not respond. His head was turned away from the man speaking to him, and his eyes were glued to the painting on the wall.

"Between the trauma of your accident and the amount of pain medication you've received, it's not unusual to have hallucinations or vivid dreams that feel very real to you." The doctor paused for a moment and waited for a response. When none came, he spoke again. "Do you understand me, Mr. Friedkin?"

Again, Malcolm remained silent.

The doctor frowned and followed Malcolm's gaze toward the painting. "If the painting disturbs you, we can remove it from the room. In fact, I think it wise considering your current state."

"No," Malcolm said. The suggestion of removing the painting stirred him. "That won't be necessary." Malcolm turned his head and looked up at the doctor. "I'm sure you are right, and I apologize for the alarm I caused the nurses."

Dr. Leonard nodded, relieved to see Malcolm acknowledging his presence. "That's fine. I just thought it might help calm you."

"Leave it," Malcolm said. "I'm a grown man, not a child suffering from nightmares of the boogeyman."

"I wasn't suggesting you were, Malcolm. Dreams and hallucinations can be quite intense. There is no shame in being alarmed by them, particularly if you've never experienced them before."

Malcolm nodded, but did not reply. He didn't want to let the painting out of his sight. He didn't want to be surprised the next time Saxan came to his room. The question was not *if* but *when*, though saying so would do him no good. This new doctor already suspected him of some sort of madness, and he did not want to encourage that.

"Very well," Doctor Leonard said. "Otherwise, your physical recovery is progressing as expected. Your memory issues should resolve in due course. Scans show no damage to your brain, other than some swelling when you arrived because of the accident that has since gone away."

"So I've been told."

The doctor frowned again. "Oh, I was unaware the nurses had passed that information on to you. It wasn't in the chart."

Malcolm smirked. *It wasn't Elaine who told me that,* he thought. *Dr. Saxan has already given me an update.*

"I'll be around to see you again before I leave today. In the meantime, rest and try to relax. Don't be hard on yourself and try to force your memories to come back. They will come on their own time, and in my experience, it's counterproductive to stress the brain trying to hurry the process."

"Yes, sir. I think I'd like to take a nap."

"Good. Sleep is how the body heals. Use the call button if you need anything, and I'll let the nurses' station know to keep a bit of an extra eye on you."

"That won't be necessary, but thank you all the same."

Dr. Leonard nodded and left the room, leaving Malcolm alone. Malcolm watched him go, then immediately turned his attention back to the painting. He wasn't sure if he was imagining it, but he thought Saxan now had the ghost of a grin on his water-color face.

By his best guess, it had been less than eight hours since the man had climbed into the painting. A fleet of nurses had rushed into his room upon his screams and found him scrambling from his bed. His IV had ripped from his arm, and several alarms were beeping from the equipment in his room. Two nurses forced him back onto the bed and pinned his arms down. Elaine had rushed back into the hall, returning a few seconds later with a syringe. She inserted the needle into his arm, and the now familiar wave of drug induced calm flowed through his veins. His screams became moans, then mumbles, then snores. Dr. Leonard had been there when he woke.

After a while, he dared to let his eyes leave the painting and turn to the whiteboard. The number thirty-seven was still written on the board.

Thirty-seven.

Malcolm closed his eyes and let the number bounce around his thoughts, hoping it would trigger a memory of something - anything. He pictured his mind as a blank canvas, like the one currently housing Saxan, and mentally painted the number on his mind. The digits were red and dripping. A final thought entered his mind as sleep came on him once again.

That doesn't look like paint. It looks like blood.

Something had changed when Malcolm opened his eyes. The room was cast in an amber glow. Bits of sky visible through the window were black and starless. The source of light was not from his room, but shining dimly through his open door. Silence was the other change. Gone were the echoing footsteps in the hallway, muffled chatter from the nurses' station, and most noticeably, the beeping of medical equipment.

He turned his head toward the tower of monitors beside his bed and found the screens black. His first thought was a power outage, though he ruled that out quickly. He was sure the hospital would have a backup generator. More than that, however, and the thing that scared him most was that he was no longer attached to the IV pole or any of the monitors. The clear tube was removed from his arm, the blood pressure cuff gone, and the EKG clips all over his upper body had been removed.

Why would they unhook everything?

In the deep silence, fear surged upon him. His fight-or-flight senses fired and adrenaline swelled. He thought once about pressing the call button for the nurses' station, but he knew it was a waste of time. There was a sinister tension in the air, and Malcolm knew it was not in his head. Something was waiting for him to make a move. At that thought, he snapped his head toward the painting, having forgotten about Dr. Saxan in the confusion of his new environment. His eyes confirmed what his mind had suspected, and it made his skin crawl.

Dr. Saxan was gone. The field was as empty as it had been upon his first waking.

"Saxan!" Malcolm's voice was still hoarse, but stronger than it had been. "I know you're here somewhere. Come out and face me." His voice echoed in the silence, but nothing stirred, and no reply came.

With no options remaining, he pushed himself up into a sitting position. His body ached at the strain, but he was relieved to find it wasn't unbearable. He fumbled with the side railing until his fingers found the button that lowered it below the frame. Gritting his teeth, he twisted and let his legs drop over the side. His bare feet touched the cold tile floor. This would be the ultimate test, but he had no choice. Mustering all his strength, he pushed with both his arms and legs and stood. His knees buckled, and for a split second, he thought he would fall. He grabbed the side rail and steadied himself. After a moment, he found he could stand without help. Cautiously, he took a single step, ready to grab back onto the railing, but he didn't need it. His legs were weak and quivered with each step, but he could walk.

Malcolm crossed the room and paused at the open doorway. Long shadows stretched away from his vision. He took a deep breath, expecting to see Dr. Saxan waiting for him in the amber glow, and stepped into the hall.

Dr. Saxan was nowhere to be seen. What he found was a hallway much longer than he expected. Doors lined both sides, and on each of them, someone had crudely painted a number in bright red paint.

Not paint. Blood.

He grimaced. Why would he think that?

Because you know it is, said the voice in his head.

The doors blurred together in his vision as he looked further down the hall until it hit a dead end and the last door. From his position, he could not make out the number painted on it, but it glowed like a beacon through the shadows.

Don't lie to yourself. You know what number is on the last door. It's thirty-seven.

"What does it mean?" Malcolm asked the empty hall.

You know what it means, said the voice.

Malcolm shuddered. The voice in his head was not his own. It was Saxan.

Go on, Malcolm. If you really don't remember, then let's see what's behind door number one.

In a daze, Malcolm approached the first door on his left. A red number one glowed against the dark wood. He grabbed the handle and pushed it open.

Behind the door was not another hospital room. It was a damp alley. The smell of garbage assaulted his senses, and he covered his nose with a trembling hand. Laying in the middle of the alley were the remains of a man. From the look of his dingy clothing, he might have been homeless. His head was busted open, and a pool of blood spread around his face. His eyes were wide and vacant.

Hmm, does he look familiar to you, Malcolm?

Malcolm turned away in disgust and slammed the door closed.

I think he does. How about we try door number two?

Malcolm didn't want to open the door, but moved across the hall, regardless. He pushed open the second door to find a motel room. The lights were off, but the television was on and white lights flashed in dizzying patterns on the wall. A woman lay on the motel bed. She was nude save for a pair of thigh high nylon stockings. Even in the flashing glow, Malcolm could see deep bruising around her neck. Her face was turned toward him, and her eyes bulged from their sockets.

What a tragic end for such a lovely young lady, wouldn't you say, Malcolm? You knew her, did you not? Quite well, if I'm not mistaken.

"No," Malcolm croaked, then closed the door. "Stop this."

I'm afraid I can't do that. There are thirty-five doors remaining. You said you wanted to remember.

One by one, Malcolm opened doors, each revealing a scene more grotesque than the last. Behind one door, he found himself on a boat. A man lay hanging over the side, his face pale, wet, and lifeless. Behind another, he found a woman hanging from a noose nearly twenty feet off the ground from a tree in a dense forest. As the numbers on the doors grew higher, the level of violence increased. Room after room of mutilated corpses and blood splattered walls. His stomach churned and more than once, he had vomited in disgust. All the while, tears streamed down his face. He had given up resistance. Begging Saxan to stop showing him these horrific scenes was futile.

At last, he came to the final door. '37' glowed vividly on the wood, as if a bright light pulsated somewhere behind it. He pushed the door open. Inside, he stood on a country road. There were no houses nearby, only fields of soybeans leaning lazily back and forth on a soft breeze. Ahead in the road, the remains of two cars were scattered everywhere. The stench of gasoline filled the air. Numbly, he walked up to what remained of the cab of the closer vehicle. He recognized it, and it did not surprise him to find he recognized the driver as well. The man behind the wheel was battered but alive. He was unconscious, but Malcolm could see the chest rising and falling in shuddering lurches.

The man in the driver's seat was Malcolm Friedkin. The car was a slate blue Chevy Impala. Malcolm's car. This was the accident that landed him in the hospital.

Another body sat in the passenger seat. This man had not fared as well as Malcolm. His body was a ruin. Deep gashes lacerated his face, chest, arms, and legs. The cab of the car was painted red with his blood. *Too much blood.* Malcolm knew this man, too. He knew the black suit and red silk shirt underneath very well. The face was mangled, but Malcolm had no trouble identifying the man.

Saxan.

Do you remember me now?

"Yes," Malcolm said aloud. His voice was dull, void of emotion.

And do you remember what you did?

"Yes."

To all of them? Each life you took?

"Yes."

I know you, Malcolm. Because of what you've done - what you did to me. I know your mind. The first was an accident. Self-defense. That homeless man attacked you. Tried to rob you. You fought back, and the man died. A justified act in the eyes of a jury of your peers. What that judge and jury did not see was how much you enjoyed it. It was a surprise for you, too. You'd never even considered the thought of taking a life. But once you did, oh Malcolm, once you had the taste of blood, you wanted more. It started slowly, right? The prostitute in the motel room? No one would miss her. Your fishing buddy you drowned on the lake? What a tragic accident. One by one, you grew more adventurous. More violent. Savoring the power of taking life. It could have gone on forever, but you made a mistake. You took chances. Killing close to other people. More danger of being caught. More thrills. Do you remember what happened when you killed me, Malcolm? I think perhaps the accident might have truly removed this last bit from your mind. Genuine memory loss. Not denial.

Malcolm did not reply. Instead, he stared dully at his own body clinging to life inside the destroyed Malibu.

The next high was killing someone on a public road in a moving car. You weren't so reckless to try it in a populated area, but the thrill was good enough to do it on a country road. How unfortunate for me to have a blowout in the middle of nowhere with no spare tire. You picked me up under the guise of a good citizen. I didn't see the knife until it was too late. Not until you buried it to the hilt in my chest. Then, as luck would have it, a car came from the other direction. So distracted in your frenzy of bloodlust, you didn't see it coming. Unfortunately for that driver, and for you, he was distracted and didn't see you swerve left of center. Miraculously, he survived, lest your number had been thirty-eight. When the police and paramedics arrived, they took you to the hospital along with the other poor fellow. They pronounced me dead at the scene. Though, it was quite obvious my injuries were not entirely caused by the accident. The police are investigating, but you won't face a jury again, Malcolm.

At least not one of your peers.

A rough hand snatched Malcolm by the back of his hospital gown, and he was lifted off the ground. He twisted and saw the disfigured face of Saxan snarling down at him, then they were moving swiftly back through the door. The blood-painted doors streaked by as they traveled down the hall. Malcolm lay still and let himself be hauled away. He knew he could not defeat Saxan, and in his heart, he knew this day would come.

Back in his room, Saxan dragged him to the corner and thrust him against the wall. His head sank into the painting and emerged into a fiery hellscape. The rest of his body followed and dropped onto a barren stone floor. He rolled to one side and looked around. The green grass and blue sky were gone, replaced with stone and jagged rocks scattered under a hazy red, smoke-filled sky. Saxan dropped through the portal beside him, then pulled him to his feet.

You will remember for all eternity, Saxan hissed. *You will remember, because I will never let you forget. You will remember in the purest way - by living it, over and over again. Thirty-seven times, again, and again.*

Saxan threw him down, and when he rolled onto his back, he was in a dark alley. Saxan stood menacingly over him, a chunk of concrete in one hand. He drew back and swung.

Malcolm remembered.

CRAWLSPACE

"**N**ope. Fuck that."

Gary frowned as the kid scrambled through the three by two feet opening, out of the crawlspace, and onto the grass.

"What's the matter? Did you see a snake in there or something, you big pussy?"

"Fuck you, old man. I'm not going back in there. I don't need this job that bad."

Gary frowned again, spat a thick wad of tobacco juice, and eyed the kid.

"What are you going on about, Paul?"

"There's some straight up devil shit down there."

"Devil shit?"

"Yeah, fucking devil shit."

Paul was a local kid with a bit of trade school, but not enough for a certificate. He was actually in his mid-twenties, but Gary considered anyone under the age of forty a kid. When Gary's partner Leroy skipped town and moved to California, Gary hired Paul to fill in. He didn't know everything, but he knew enough to get by. Until now, he'd proven reliable. Sure, he showed up to a few morning jobs so hungover he could barely open his eyes, but he showed up. He never refused a job either, no matter how much shit they had to crawl through to find the busted pipe. Not until now.

"Kid, I'm not following you here. What exactly did you see?"

"I crawled to the main line to check it out, and I saw a red glow further back under the house. Never seen a red glowing light under a house before, so I crawled back in there to see what it was. I get back there, and they've got some kind of devil shrine or some shit. Inverted crosses drawn on the ground, black candles, little statues, weird shit."

Gary spit again as he considered. "You pullin' my leg, kid? We've got three jobs today. No time to be goofing off."

Paul shook his head. "No, sir. I don't know what kind of shit these people are into, but I'm not messing around with it."

Gary turned and took a few steps to peek around the corner of the house. He didn't know the people who lived here, but the guy who called in with a drainage problem sounded normal enough. The house was in a typical upscale neighborhood—well manicured lawn and flower beds, nice cars, and boats or campers in about every other driveway. Nothing to suggest any devil shit. At least not like you see on tv.

"Alright, kid. Maybe these folks are into some weird shit, but that's their business, not ours. Our business is getting their plumbing back in working order. We'll do what we have to do, pay no mind to whatever they got going on under the house, and go on our merry way. Does that work for you?"

Paul gritted his teeth and looked back at the crawl space opening. "I don't like it, man. And I'm damn sure not going back in there by myself."

"Fine, I'll go in with you. I'd probably have to, anyway. The day you can handle a job on your own will be the day I retire."

"Fuck you, old man," Paul said again, but this time there was a relief in his voice.

Gary winked at Paul and then dropped down to his knees with an audible grunt. "Let's see what we got here, shall we?"

He poked his head into the crawlspace, and the musty smell of wet earth and sewage assaulted him. He grimaced, then pushed forward, his shoulders barely scraping through the opening. *Getting too old and too fat for this bullshit.* He crawled further in, then turned to make sure Paul followed him. As he waited, he noticed the red glow on the opposite side of the crawlspace. A nervous sensation ran over him, and he suddenly didn't care much for being down here alone.

"Hurry up, Paul," he shouted. "Let's get this over with."

Paul poked his head into the crawlspace and locked eyes with Gary.

"You feel it too, don't you?" Paul asked. "Something fucking weird."

"I don't feel shit except claustrophobic, so let's get this done and get out of here," Gary snapped back, though the words rang hollow in his mind. He felt what the kid was talking about. It felt *wrong.*

Gary led the way, and they crawled deeper under the house. Their hands and knees sank in the soft ground, giving wet sucking sounds with each movement. They followed the drainage pipes to the mainline connecting to the sewer system. The smell of raw sewage was overwhelming the closer they got. The ground grew muddy and Gary saw wads of used toilet paper scattered around the pipe. His stomach lurched, and he held his breath for a moment, trying to shut down his olfactory senses. Paul gagged behind him.

Gary fished a couple of packs of foam plugs from his pocket and handed one back to Paul. "Shove these up your nose," he said, panting from a mix of exertion and trying to not breathe through his nose. He opened the other pack and pushed the foam plugs deep into his nostrils. The smell faded, though he swore he could still taste the putrid air.

Paul moved up beside him and aimed a flashlight at the pipe. A large section was busted open and gray water filled the pipe, dripping out onto the dirt.

"God damn," Gary said. This was going to be a significant job. Replacing the mainline was not a quick fix.

"How the hell did that happen?" Paul asked.

"Pressure," Gary answered. "There must be a bitch of a clog in that line, and all the pressure blew the pipe."

"Never seen one that bad," Paul said.

Gary grunted, but didn't speak. Truth be told, he'd never seen one that bad either. It didn't look like a pressure blow out. It looked like someone had smashed the damn thing with a rock.

"Alright," Gary said. "Let's get out of this mess, and I'll call the owner and deliver the bad news. This one's not gonna be cheap."

Paul nodded, eager to get out of the crawlspace. He turned to retreat to the opening, but a loud scraping sound caused him to jerk back. The noise came from the back corner near the red glow. Both men watched as a bright square of light appeared on the ground beside the shrine. There was a shuffling noise, and then a large black sack of some sort fell into the crawlspace. The scraping sound returned and the square of light disappeared.

"Holy shit," Paul wheezed.

Gary didn't respond. His eyes were glued to the black sack that lay on the floor across the crawlspace. It was moving.

"We gotta get outta here, man," Paul whispered. His eyes were wide with fear, and he tugged on Gary's shirt sleeve.

"There's something in that bag," Gary said, still not taking his eyes from it.

"I don't care. I want out of here."

"Look at it, Paul. You know what's in it, same as I do. There's someone in that bag."

Paul looked at the bag again and moaned. "Holy shit."

Gary crawled toward the bag, but Paul yanked him back.

"What the fuck are you doing, old man?"

"We can't just leave somebody tied up in a bag," Gary hissed. "They'll suffocate."

"No, no, no, no," Paul said. "I'm getting out of here. Somebody threw that sack down here through a hatch, Gary. That means someone is home, and they know we're down here. This is fucked, man. I'm getting out."

Gary watched Paul scramble back toward the opening to the back yard.

"I'll get to the truck and call the cops," he shouted back.

Gary shook his head and continued to crawl to the back corner toward the squirming bag. He could hear faint moans from inside. His gut was an icy slush, but he moved on pure adrenaline. Whoever was in that bag needed help. He couldn't live with himself if he left them down there and something happened.

"FUCK!"

Gary stopped and turned back. Paul was at the edge of the crawlspace, but the access window was gone, cloaking the area in darkness. Paul slapped at the wood blocking the exit, but it wouldn't budge. He twisted around so his legs were toward the wood, then kicked with both feet. The sound echoed in the crawlspace, but the wood held.

"We're fucking trapped, Gary," Paul shouted. He was near hysterics, and his voice choked with emotion.

Gary felt panic rising within him, but he fought it. If they were going to get out of this, he would have to keep a clear head.

"Come over here," he called across the crawlspace. "If we can't get out that way, we'll get out through the hatch into the house."

Paul scrambled across the floor, slapping in the mud. His fear of being trapped had conquered his fear of the strange shrine and the sack, which now bucked in response to the commotion. Gary moved beside him, and they covered the distance in seconds.

When they reached the sack, Gary pulled out his pocket knife and grabbed a handful of the heavy cloth. He pulled it away from the body, careful not to cut the person inside, and sliced the sack open.

A woman stared up at him, her eyes frantic. She had been gagged with duct tape wrapped around her mouth. Gary ripped the cloth apart with both hands to free the rest of her. Her hands and feet were bound with white zip ties. He took her hands, trying not to frighten her anymore than she already was, and cut the ties. She reached up and peeled the tape from her mouth, spitting a wad of cloth onto the floor. She gasped, then wrapped her arms around Gary.

"They're gonna kill me," she whispered. She panted in his ear and clung to him in desperation.

"Who did this to you?" Gary asked.

"I don't know," she said. "They were wearing masks. They took me. I was leaving the mall, and they took me." She cried, and Gary held her tight against him.

"It's gonna be okay," he whispered. "We're gonna get you out of here, right Paul? Paul?"

Gary turned to Paul for reassurance, but the kid was staring at the shrine. Gary followed his gaze and saw what had transfixed Paul.

The ground was moving. The inverted crosses drawn on the ground surged up and down as the dirt shifted. Gary realized he could feel a vibration resonating from beneath. The girl noticed at the same time.

"What is that?" she cried.

A shrill squeal sounded throughout the crawl space causing all three of them to flinch away and cover their ears. An amplified voice sounded from speakers that seemed to be placed all around them.

We present you this sacrifice so that you might show us favor in the days to come. We offer three—the wise man, the reckless youth, and the virgin. Feast to your satisfaction and shower us with good fortune. We pray to you, our dark lord.

The speakers fell silent, and the ground rumbled. The vibration caused the black candles and demonic statues to tip and fall. Dirt shifted and raised up, sending small rocks and chunks of mud tumbling to the side. Gary scrambled backward, pulling the girl with him. Paul sat still, tears flowing down his cheeks as he watched the ground open up.

A pair of yellow eyes appeared first, the red lights glistening off snake-like pupils. Then scale covered arms rippling with lean muscle emerged from the dirt, and the creature erupted from the ground at lightning speed. Paul didn't react before the monster slashed his throat open with a savage claw, sending blood spraying across the crawl space. He collapsed onto his back and the creature was on him, ripping and tearing at the wound, blood and meat flinging in all directions.

The girl screamed and crawled away from Gary and the hideous beast. The thing snapped to attention at her scream and crawled on all fours like an alligator after her. Gary sat in stunned silence as the beast caught her and ended her screams. He couldn't bear to look, but he heard the butchery happening behind him.

As he waited for the creature to finish the girl and come for him, he thought of his old partner Leroy. He was sitting on a beach somewhere looking out at the Pacific. Gary had been furious at Leroy for bailing on their company and leaving him to deal with it. Now he was happy Leroy got out. Best decision he ever made. That was for damn sure.

Gary heard the soft pats of the creature's clawed hands sinking into the mud, and he braced himself for what was to come. His eyes fell on the demonic symbols now scattered around the crawlspace, and he said a prayer of his own.

Dear God, let this be quick.

A guttural chuckle sounded just behind him.

"He's not listening," the creature said.

Gary's heart hammered in his chest, but he fought off the urge to scream. Instead, he seized the moment, however brief it would be, and spoke to the creature. "How about you? Do you listen?"

"I hear everything."

"I've got a question for you," Gary said. His voice quivered with fear, but he pressed on. "Why do you let those people upstairs control you?"

The creature chuckled again, sending ripples of goosebumps over Gary's body.

"They control nothing."

"Seems to me like you come when they call for you, and then ask for your blessings. Seems to me like they're using you. How many of them are up there? You must know, right?"

The creature paused, snorted, and then answered. "Four."

"Well," Gary said, feigning confidence, "the way I see it, you can eat me, and then crawl back into your hole until they decide they need you again. Or you can bust open that hatch and feast on the four of them. Your call."

The demon crawled around Gary until they faced each other. The beast's snout hovered inches from Gary's face. Blood and chunks of meat smeared the creature's teeth, and Gary was thankful he still had the foam plugs up his nose.

"You are a wise man," the creature said. "I like how you think, and I am so very hungry." The creature reached up a claw and hooked it under Gary's chin. "Perhaps we will meet again."

Before Gary could respond, the creature twisted and darted across the crawlspace. It threw its body into the hatch, sending shrapnel into the room above. Gary heard a startled shout. The creature jumped through the hatch opening and disappeared from view. Screams filled the air.

Gary crawled to the hatch and hoisted himself up into the house. The walls were a tapestry of carnage and pieces of bodies lay scattered. In a daze, he walked from room to room until he came to the front door. He heard the sickening crunch of bones in a nearby room, but he did not dare look. He stepped out onto the porch and closed the door behind him, crossed the yard, and climbed into his truck. A lot of thoughts went through his mind as he stared out the windshield. None of them were good.

He took a last look at the house. Nothing on the exterior suggested the horror that waited inside. Gary decided he'd had enough. He started the engine and backed the truck out onto the road. He thought again of Leroy, who had the good sense to walk away. Now it was Gary's turn.

He pointed the truck west and chased the sun all the way to the Pacific.

An Angel in the Dark

Mission Briefing:

On January 21st, 2087, the space shuttle Metropolis 2 launched a fifteen year voyage to chart, observe, and determine habitability of planets in neighboring galaxies through use of wormhole space travel technologies. Eleven years into the journey, we received a distress signal on Earth from the Metropolis. The ship had engaged an automated abort mission procedure and returned to our galaxy, emerging from a wormhole between Jupiter and Mars. It is unknown how long it has been since the ship's abort sequence began as the distress signal could not reach Earth until the ship returned to our solar system. Files retrieved with the distress signal show a critical incident must have occurred onboard the ship. Only one potential survivor remains onboard the Metropolis, known because of entries in the ship's voyage logs by Logan Vanerich. Mr. Vanerich is the ship's dietician. Through these entries, we have some insight into the events leading to the aborted mission, though the entries suggest Mr. Vanerich suffered a mental break and we deem his reports unreliable. Since returning to the solar system, there has been no response from the ship. We have launched rescue vessels with supplies to dock with the Metropolis and attempt to retrieve Mr. Vanerich and any other potential survivors. The voyage logs entered by Logan Vanerich are attached to this missive for your review. We will provide an update when the rescue vessels dock, sixty-seven days from this writing.

Admiral Trent Savage

Metropolis Travel Log: Entry 421A - User: Logan Vanerich

This is a distress call. My name is Logan Vanerich, and I am onboard the Metropolis 2 spacecraft. I don't know my current coordinates. I hope the ship's systems are functioning, and my location is being broadcast along with my message, though I do not know how that works. Also, I don't know if anyone will receive this message. The Metropolis 2 mission is to explore distant galaxies in search of habitable planets. We've gone through multiple wormholes over the last decade. If this signal ever reaches Earth, I think it will have gone on quite the journey.

Anyway, the distress call. Right. Forgive me for not following standard messaging protocols and formats. Writing this like I'm talking to someone is giving me a small bit of peace. Indulge me, if you will.

After ten years onboard the Metropolis, I lost my shit. Isolation, claustrophobia, panic attacks, the whole nine. All of us did plenty of prep work and testing pre-launch to make sure we were ready for the harshness of space travel. Sorry to say, but there is nothing you can do on Earth to prepare yourself for space. I made it ten years before I cracked. For my money, that ain't bad.

When it got to the point of *we have to do something about this*, the ship's medical team stepped in and Doc Merriman gave me the full scan. He told me what I already knew—the mental strain of deep space travel was wearing me down and my condition was declining. His recommendation was temporary cryogenic stasis. Stick me in the freeze tube and let me nap in suspended animation for a month or two. I was onboard. There was no way for me to get off the ship, so the next best thing was tapping out and taking a long nap. Doc said I would still have some symptoms when I woke up, but they would be less severe after giving my body and mind a chance to rest. I agreed with the treatment plan and entered a stasis chamber programmed to shut down and release me in thirty-five days.

That was thirty-six days ago.

Yesterday, I woke up.

Everyone is gone. I've searched every inch of the ship a dozen times. There's no one here, and nothing to explain where they went. We're in space. You can't go outside. There is nowhere they could have gone. But they're gone. All of them.

So, yeah, distress. I am in distress.

I'll keep searching the ship for some clue as to what happened. It's the only thing I can do. I will upload reports as things develop.

I hope someone is receiving this. I don't know if it's even possible from this distance, but it's the only shot I've got.

Mayday, mayday, Metropolis 2 needs immediate assistance.

Metropolis Travel Log: Entry 421B - User: Logan Vanerich

It's been two days since my first report. Still no sign of any other crewmates. I've been trying to review flight logs and captain's notes, but I don't know what I'm looking at. Of all the people onboard to end up stranded alone, it had to be me. It had to be the least technically savvy guy in all of space.

The fucking cook.

I'd apologize for my language, but does it really matter? Something tells me no one will ever see this, or if they do, it will be long after I've either died of starvation or launched myself into space in a fit of madness.

Madness. I already feel it creeping in. I thought the isolation of space was bad before. Jesus Christ, I had no idea. It's only been two days, but I'd sell my soul to talk to someone.

I'm getting off track. Sorry, I've been doing that a lot. The captain's logs. After scanning the system for a while, I found the trip logs. Real tedious stuff. Lot of coordinates and travel plans. Wormhole math I don't have the slightest idea how to interpret. I flunked out of calculus in college. Flunked out of college altogether. That's how I ended up in culinary school. I don't know the derivative of 2x+3, but I can make a damn good omelet. I guess they needed somebody like that. Somebody to keep the comforts of home alive in this endless void. I know there are infinite possibilities out there, but from where I'm sitting, it looks like an endless nothing.

I'm losing it again. Fucking omelets. Jesus, what am I doing?

The flight logs are all time stamped, but we've been up here for ten years, so there's a shit ton of them. I haven't figured out a way to search yet, so I'm just scrolling through. Everything had been routine until I went into stasis, so far as I know at least, so I'm trying to find that point and start from there. It may be a waste of time. Who knows if they had time to document what happened? My guess is not. But, it seems that time is pretty much all I've got right now. Plenty of it to waste.

I'll report back soon. I kind of like talking to you. Makes me feel not so alone.

Metropolis Travel Log: Entry 421C - User: Logan Vanerich

I'm back. I think it's the day after my last entry, but I'm having a hard time keeping track of time. My sleep comes in short bursts, and I can't exactly count on the sun to tell me the time of day.

I've scrolled all the way to the captain's log entries from when I went into stasis. It includes a short little snippet about me. In the middle of a deep space exploration mission, they took the time to make a brief mention of my mental breakdown. I'm flattered. According to reports, Crewmate Vanerich (that's me) is suffering from psychological fatigue and stress due to the isolation of space travel. His (my) condition is declining steadily and medical personnel agree a stasis sleep is the best approach. It also notes that should stasis fail to alleviate the symptoms in Crewmate Vanerich, further measures, up to and including drug induced sedation and confinement, may be necessary.

They didn't tell me that part.

It's okay, though. Kind of wish I could find those drugs they were going to sedate me with. I could use something to take the edge off. I'm hearing things. Space is quiet, and the ship doesn't make much noise other than the hum of electronics and air ventilation. After a while, those sounds become white noise, and you don't even hear them anymore. When any other sound comes, it's quite noticeable. It has to be coming from inside the ship. It's not like the neighbors are having a barbecue and have the radio up a little too loud.

Barbecue. I'd kill for a nice pulled pork sandwich right about now. Space food kinda sucks, which is sad to say since I'm the cook. It's not my fault, though. I have limited options, and I can't use actual flame to heat anything. Fire on a spaceship is frowned upon.

Anyway, my reading is caught up now and the story I've titled *What the Fuck Happened to Everybody Else and other Mysteries* is about to begin. You'd think I would dive straight into it once I got there, but I wanted to let you know about it first. It felt like an achievement worth sharing with someone, and you are all I have. Also, it makes sense to take a few minutes to celebrate, because I'm more than a little concerned that I won't find any answers in the remaining travel logs. The idea that someone would take the time to document whatever emergency occurred to remove dozens of people from a deep space voyage is wishful thinking at its absolute boldest. I think I'm going to come away disappointed and with no other path to follow than madness.

Is it so bad to want to celebrate just for a moment? I don't think so. I hope you aren't judging me for it. In fact, isn't this a hook to keep you reading? Don't you want to find out what happened, too? I think I would if I were on the other end of this screen.

On that note, I'm off to see what there is to see. Sit tight and cross your fingers for me. Send me good vibes. Pray if you pray. I don't know what I believe, but none of those things can hurt. I believe that.

Over and out.

I always wanted to say that.

Metropolis Travel Log: 421D - User: Logan Vanerich

Hey! I'm back. I hope things are going well for you. I'm as well as can be, considering my situation. You know my situation, right? I guess I took it for granted that the same person would read each of my messages. If you're joining right in the middle, this won't make a lick of sense. But, though I do have the time, I don't want to recap the entire situation with every entry. That would be a disservice to you if you are the same person reading each entry. Redundant with a capital R. I'm going to keep with the trend and assume you're caught up on the story. I'll spare you the "Previously on What the Fuck Happened to Everyone Else and Other Mysteries" recap. If you're new, I suggest you scroll back and read from the beginning.

Now that we've cleared that up, I have not returned empty-handed. To my delight, there were indeed some log entries of an unusual nature. Shortly after I entered stasis, the ship detected an *anomaly* in the distance. The report calls it a *foreign body with no discernible identification*. Even more intriguing, the object does not appear on any scans of the area. The computer says nothing is there, but everyone can see it.

What a mystery! The game is afoot! I always wanted to say that, too. I wonder if Sir Arthur Conan Doyle ever imagined that hundreds of years in the future his work would be referenced in deep space. It should be. Sherlock Holmes is one of the greatest fictional characters of all time, if I do say so myself. I wish he was here with me. I don't have the brainpower to be Sherlock, but I like to think I'd make a fine Watson.

Right, anomaly in space, no radar detection, visible only to the naked eye. Stay on track. The log says the object was more or less in the same direction the ship was traveling. It did not appear to be moving, so the decision was made to continue course and investigate further as the ship neared the object.

The captain must have thought little of it, because the next few entries were standard reports of ship status. Then, we get to the really good stuff. The next report states that the object is now within fifty miles of the ship, and it has begun to move. Radar still does not register the object, but visual reports describe it as a white mist that appears to be undulating slowly. Undulating, that's a good word. Makes me think of an octopus blobbing around in the ocean, undulating through the currents. No doubt that is how Sherlock Holmes would describe it. The object is moving toward the ship, which is an odd occurrence, wouldn't you say? It wasn't moving before, but started moving toward the ship when it got closer. I don't know about you, but that suggests intelligence to me. Deductive reasoning.

Is it an alien?

Wouldn't that be something? A decade of traveling across the void of space, and we have yet to come across anything suggesting alien life. Although, I would argue our undulating friend seems to fit the bill. If the captain thought so, he chose not to put it in the report. I suppose I can't blame him. Best not to get carried away and make assumptions.

So, now we're on high alert. We don't know what this thing is, but we all agree it is unusual and unlike anything we've come across on our voyage. The game is afoot, indeed!

I stopped here to come and give you an update. There is only one more entry in the captain's log. That's not a good sign. You can't imagine how difficult it was for me not to dive into that last log entry. It just wouldn't have been fair to you. What if what I read is so dreadful that I cannot bear to write it again? I couldn't leave you hanging like that. No, we're in this together. You and me.

I'll be back soon. I've been awake for a very long time, and I need to rest, but I can't put this off any longer. Stay tuned, my friend. You are my friend, aren't you? I hope so.

Metropolis Travel Log: 421E - User: Logan Vanerich

Well, that was anticlimactic. I guess it lines up with what I suspected. Whatever happened must have happened quickly, leaving no time for the crew to document the facts of the case. The anomaly approached the ship, didn't set off any proximity alarms, and held position alongside us, matching our speed. After that, it didn't do anything. Just cruised along with us. The report states the anomaly still moved in a fluid manner (undulating, remember?), and some crew members claim to have witnessed the thing forming recognizable shapes. If that's not intelligent actions, I don't know what is. This thing was an alien lifeform.

Was it, though? We're not in our neck of the universe anymore. Doesn't that make us aliens, now? No wonder this thing floated over and hitched a ride. If an unknown alien life form came riding through your space, you'd want to investigate, wouldn't you? I know I would.

It's besides the point, I suppose. Nothing else happened, and the captain was at a loss. The last piece of the report stated they were preparing to use one of the exploring arms and attempt to touch the anomaly.

That was the final entry in the captain's log.

I'm gonna wager the plan to reach out and touch it did not go well.

Now, here we are, more or less back where we started. I'm on this ship alone and I still don't know what happened to everyone else. Got to admit, I feel pretty defeated. Going through the captain's logs gave me a purpose. I suspected it would end this way, but I didn't *know*. That bit of hope kept me going. That hope is extinguished now, and I have no direction.

I can't just mope around and wait to die. What would Sherlock do? Let's consider what we know. The captain used the ship's arm to touch or interact with the anomaly. Since there is no further report and everyone is gone, it's safe to say that was a bad idea. But why? What could have happened to lead to this result? We must assume the anomaly is intelligent and likely had negative intentions. Or would it have had any intention at all, other than its natural instincts? There are two scenarios, one of those having two results. Both scenarios are based on the idea that by touching it, the anomaly could gain access to the ship.

One, the anomaly came on board, was intelligent and well intentioned. Perhaps it carried everyone to another place, leaving me behind because it didn't know I was here. I find this unlikely. Maybe I'm a pessimist, but I can't see a friendly alien running into us and transporting everybody to a paradise.

Two, the anomaly came on board and eradicated everyone. It could have done this by natural instinct with no consciousness behind it, or it could have been aggressive. Either way, I was left behind because it didn't know I was here.

I have seen no signs of any other life forms, so I feel confident saying whatever it was is now gone.

I need to think. I need to sleep.

Goodnight, friend. Maybe tomorrow I'll have an epiphany.

Metropolis Travel Log: 421F - User: Logan Vanerich

Hello, again. Sorry it's been so long. I think it's been about a week, but I don't know for sure. Could've been a couple of days. Everything is running together.

I've got nothing. I guess that's why I didn't want to write. You're counting on me to figure this thing out, and I don't even have the slightest of leads. The anomaly is likely gone forever, and there's a high probability that the Metropolis is going to drift through space until it smashes into something. I don't know how to change our course. I can't influence the ship. If only someone else was here who knew how to activate wormhole travel and pop us back into our own solar system, preferably close to earth.

I want to go home.

That's pretty much all I think about anymore. I'd give anything to set my feet back on earth and breathe fresh air again. I want to see people again. I always considered myself a bit of an introvert, but spend some time in my shoes and you'll become the biggest people-person in the universe. You are all I have left.

That's all I've got right now. Sorry I'm not more cheerful. Listening to my misery must be draining for you. I don't mean to be a burden.

Talk to you later.

Metropolis Travel Log: 421G - User: Logan Vanerich

I'm thinking about ending this. I can't go on like this forever. I'm not going to starve, and who knows how long the ship can drift. Even if the ship fails, what would happen? We're in infinite space. We'll just fall or float or drift until we hit something. That could take lifetimes to happen.

I can't do this anymore.

I'm sorry I've let you down. My personal information is on file some-where back on Earth. If you can, please let my family know that I did the best I could, and I'm sorry.

I'm so sorry.

Metropolis Travel Log: 421H - User: Logan Vanerich

You won't believe what happened! It came back. The anomaly. It's out there, so far I almost missed it, but it's there. I was at the rear hatch of the ship. My plan was to open the hatch without a spacesuit. I figured it was the fastest way to, you know, take care of it? I have a low tolerance for pain, so I wanted to do something quick. A walk outside the ship would do the trick.

As you might imagine, I was struggling with cold feet. It's a scary thing to pull the plug on yourself, especially if you don't have any firm beliefs about what might come after. While I was trying to work up the nerve, I kept looking out the hatch window, and that's when I saw it. And do you know what? It saw me.

I know, you must be saying to yourself, "how does he know that"? Believe me, I get it. I would ask the same question. I don't have a good answer for it, either. I just know. There's a connection between us. I feel it.

It's hard to tell for sure, but I think it's moving closer. I think it's coming to me.

That's all for now. I'm afraid to be away from the window for too long. I don't want to lose it. I'll be back when I know more.

Metropolis Travel Log: 421I - User: Logan Vanerich

It's a girl. The anomaly. It's a girl, and she's beautiful. When I returned to the window, she was much closer. I could make out a lot more details. No doubt she is what the crew saw while I was asleep. She moves like a ghost; twisting and swirling in and out of focus. Undulating, just like we talked about before.

I know what you're thinking. This guy has lost it. I don't blame you for feeling that way. Let me explain. I didn't make the connection right away. When the anomaly was still a distance away, I thought of it much like my crewmates must have, albeit with a bit more sense of concern knowing what I know about the fate of the crew. It was when it came all the way up to the window. That's when I knew the truth. That's when I saw her face.

You heard me right; her face. Even though her body is constantly morphing and fading, she has a humanoid shape. Not human, but humanoid. She's too beautiful to be human. The way she looks at me through the glass, I can't do justice. There is such empathy and understanding in her eyes. She knows my pain, my struggle. I think she knows these things because she feels them, too. She understands me, because she is me. Lost in space. All we want is to be together. I just have to let her in.

She's waiting for me. I have to go.

Metropolis Travel Log: 421J - User: Logan Vanerich

It's taken a long time, and I nearly gave up, but I figured out how to do it. I know how to let her in. She's been so patient and encouraging. I've studied the control room menus, and I can manually open the rear hatch. I must make sure the inner chamber is completely sealed, or else I might kill myself in the process. Funny how that was exactly what I wanted to do just a short while ago. Now, I'm terrified at the thought of my life ending without being together with her.

I think I know what I'm doing. I explained my plan to her through the window and she smiled, so it must be a good plan. I can't wait any longer.

I'm letting her in.

Metropolis Travel Log: 421K - User: ***Unverified User - Biometric scan indicates user Logan Vanerich - 92% match***

I don't understand what's happening. She was so close. Right there outside the window. I saw her face. It was the most beautiful thing I've ever seen. I ran back to the control room and activated the spacewalk hatch. I watched the monitors, waiting for her to come inside. The sooner she was in, the sooner I could close the hatch and go to her. But she never came inside. I waited as long as I could stand it, then I closed the hatch and ran back to the window.

She was gone. I don't see her anywhere. She could be below the ship, or at an angle I can't see from any of the port windows, but why? Why would she hide from me? She wanted to come in. I felt it.

I don't feel well. I need to lie down. My heart is broken.

Why would she leave me?

Metropolis Travel Log: 421L - ***Unverified User - Biometric scan indicates user Logan Vanerich - 86% match. Biometric scanning system fault suspected. Rebooting***

This is torture. I can hear her calling for me, but I can't find her. She sounds so far away, like an echo in my mind. Sometimes it sounds like she is inside the ship. How else could I be hearing her? I've searched everywhere, and her voice never seems to be any closer.

I have to go. My nose is bleeding and I'm so tired.

Metropolis Travel Log: 421M - ***Unverified User - System corrupted***

Something is happening to me. My whole body aches. I'm having violent cramps and my nose keeps bleeding. I have a splitting headache. I can barely look at this screen. Sometime today blood came out of my ear. Blood is coming out of other places, too. Places I don't want to mention.

I'm scared. She's getting louder. But I don't think I want to be with her anymore. Sometimes I feel like she's in my head, and her calls aren't coming from in the ship or outside. I think they're in my head.

Metropolis Travel Log: 421N - ***Biometric user scanning deactivated***

She's here.

Metropolis Autopilot - Deactivated

Manual Course Adjustment

Wormhole Activated

Portal Breach Complete

New Location - Home Solar System

Metropolis Travel Log: 421O - User: Logan Vanerich

Command center, please respond. This is Logan Vanerich requesting emergency extraction and return to Earth. I am the sole survivor. A viral contagion infected the entire crew while I was in stasis. All crew members were deceased upon my releases from stasis. To protect myself from the contagion, I ejected all the remains from the ship and ran sanitization protocols. I show no signs of infection. Bio scans are clear. Disregard prior travel log entries registered under my name. One of the crew must have hacked the system to impersonate me and make bizarre entries while under the effects of the contagion.

Command center, please respond. I repeat, Logan Vanerich requesting emergency extraction.

I must return to Earth.

1 BUY OLD MARBLES

"Holy shit! Did you see that?"

Brennan pulled the beer can from between his legs in the driver's seat and chugged the rest in two large swallows. "See what?" He looked up at the rear-view mirror to see Riley cackling in the back seat.

Tyler twisted in the passenger seat and reached back behind the driver's seat, fishing two more cans of beer from the open case on the floorboard. He handed a fresh one to Brennan, then cracked open his. "What are you talking about?"

Riley laughed again and pointed his thumb back down the road in the direction they had come. "That sign back there on the tree. Did you see it?"

"No," Brennan said.

"There was a sign nailed to a tree back there that said, 'I buy old marbles'." Riley erupted into another fit of laughter and sloshed beer all over his lap.

"Hey, don't spill beer on my seats, bro," Brennan shouted, uselessly scolding his drunken companion.

That got Riley and Tyler laughing, and then Brennan followed suit. The whole car smelled like a brewery. Brennan knew if they got pulled over, they were fucked. But, even though they didn't know the roads in the area well, he was confident the odds of running into a cop were pretty slim. They weren't quite the back roads he was used to back home in Indiana, but pretty damn close.

It was strange to have a prestigious university nestled in the middle of nowhere, but it had its perks. They could load up on booze and leave town, then five minutes later they were cruising the middle of rural nowhere. All the cops were back in town busting underage college kids dumb enough to wander around while drunk off their asses. Tyler had just turned twenty-one a month before, now allowing their little group to buy a case and hit the privacy of the back roads. They partook in their fair share of dorm parties, but Brennan was a country boy at heart. He enjoyed getting buzzed and going out to the quiet places away from the lights. He had minor misgivings about drinking and driving, but he felt in control, and there was never much traffic on roads like these.

"We gotta go back," Riley said. "I have to meet the guy who buys old marbles."

"Fuck that," Tyler said. "Probably some kid. Why would an adult buy marbles?"

"No way it's a kid," Riley replied. "Kids don't play with marbles. My little brother doesn't even know what a marble is. They play Fortnite and shit now. That's it. Little fuckers don't even go outside anymore."

"Fair point," Brennan said. "People collect all kinds of shit. This guy must be into steel balls." He laughed, cueing the other two to crack up again.

"You got any marbles to sell them?" Tyler asked, twisted in his seat again.

"Got two big ones right here," Riley said, cupping his crotch.

"He said marbles, not pebbles," Brennan said.

"Good one, dipshit," Riley said with a chuckle. "I don't have marbles, but I bet the dollar store does."

"I'm not going to a fucking dollar store. And if I did, and if they had marbles, I wouldn't knock on some stranger's door offering to sell him a sack of marbles," Brennan said.

"Why not? He has a sign. What else do you need? Come on, man! It's not even nine o'clock yet."

Tyler shook his head, but he had an amused smile on his face. "They wouldn't be old marbles, though."

"We can roll them around in the dirt. Scuff them up a little. Come on! There's a dollar store on every fucking corner these days. I bet we can find one in less than ten minutes without going back to school. All these little towns have them now. It's like Walmart for towns too small to have a Walmart."

Brennan smirked. It was a stupid idea, but Riley's enthusiasm, along with the building buzz, made it intriguing.

Riley grabbed his phone, the white screen glowing in the back seat, and tapped on the screen. Then a computerized voice sounded from the speaker.

"Starting route to Dollar General. In 2.8 miles, turn left."

All three men busted out laughing. In 2.8 miles, Brennan turned left.

A half hour later, the three young men were heading back the way they'd come, equipped with a torn open sack of marbles. They were the cheap, plastic kind with colorful swirls trapped inside. Riley had taken a ridiculous amount of pleasure in rubbing them around in the dirt and grass beside the dollar store parking lot, while Brennan and Tyler nodded and waved at shoppers passing through to and from their cars. Brennan and Tyler both laughed when one middle-aged woman put an arm around her young son and steered him away from the boys. She gave a disgusted sneer at the intoxicated men and shook her head.

"Don't grow up to be like us," Tyler had called to the boy.

With Riley satisfied that they could not age the marbles any more, they loaded back into the car and left the store. Brennan was wary of potential small-town police, but the store was on the edge of town, and they had escaped unseen.

As they got closer to the house with the bizarre sign seeking old marbles, Brennan grew uneasy. Despite all the beers fueling this foolishness, it was starting to feel like a bad idea.

"You guys sure about this?"

Riley leaned up between the front seats. "What do you mean? This is gonna be hilarious. Why *wouldn't* we be sure?"

"We've been drinking, man. You don't think it's going to set off a bunch of red flags for this guy when three intoxicated guys show up at his house to sell him marbles? What if he's got a gun or something? This is a rural area, man. Everybody has guns in places like this. Or what if he calls the cops? Drinking and driving on top of being underaged will not look good on my record."

"All fair points," Tyler said, sipping another beer.

"We already bought the marbles though," Riley said, as if that sufficed as a point of no return.

"They were two bucks," Brennan said. "I'll pay you back."

"I don't want two dollars. I want to flip them for more and meet this dude." Riley threw back the rest of his beer and cracked another open. "We'll behave."

Tyler snorted laughter. "Yeah, totally presentable."

Brennan shook his head.

"Look, we'll check it out, and if things seem like they might go sideways, we'll bail out. Even if he calls the cops, we'll be long gone before they get out here. Park away from the house a little, so it's hard to see the license plate." Riley looked out the window, then twisted to the back window. "There it was! And there was a light on in the front window. Turn around and go back."

Brennan debated, but in the end, drunken curiosity defeated instinct and he turned the car around at a gravel drive a quarter mile past the house. Back on the road, they approached the house. This time, Brennan saw the sign for himself. It was wooden and painted white. *I Buy Old Marbles* was stenciled across the top, and below that were a few hand-painted marbles. He also saw Riley had been right about the lights being on. A dull glow shone through the front window of the house. Flickers of blue light that must have been a tv flashed on the portion of wall visible from the front of the house.

Brennan steered into the driveway and shut down the car. He took a deep breath and turned to the other two. "For real, if this gets weird, we're out. And don't be assholes. I don't like this, but we're here now. Be respectful."

Riley threw a thumbs up and flashed a wide smile. He shoved the handful of marbles into his jacket pocket and climbed out of the car.

Tyler opened the door and laughed. "This is the dumbest thing I've ever done, and I've done some dumb shit."

Brennan kept quiet. Now that he was out of the car and approaching the front door, all his misgivings had returned, and his gut feeling was to turn right back around and get out of here. He almost said so, but Riley rushed forward as if he suspected Brennan was about to back down, and knocked on the door.

Brennan cringed at the noise, but it was too late now. With his gut churning, he stood by his friends and waited for someone to answer.

Brennan wasn't sure what to expect of the person who answered the door, but it wasn't the frail, haggard old man who stood before them, peering at the strangers crowded around his doorstep.

"Help you boys?"

Brennan couldn't seem to find the right words to say, and his mouth hung ajar.

"We saw your sign, sir," Riley chimed in. He fished into his jacket pocket.

The old man stiffened, unsure what the young man had in his pocket. Brennan felt a pang of guilt, realizing the old man thought Riley had a weapon of some sort. Then Riley held out a handful of marbles, and the old man's face lit up. His eyes widened in surprise, and he smiled.

"Marbles! Come inside, boys. Come inside!" He stepped back and motioned them toward the small living room.

The men shuffled in and took in the quaint house. There was nothing unusual about it. The furniture was dated, and the air smelled musty. It reminded Brennan of his own grandparents' house back in Indiana, and he felt a wave of shame. He would be horrified to find out three drunk college kids had barged in on his grandparents unannounced and was embarrassed to be taking part in this scheme.

"Yeah, we saw your sign and just happened to have some old marbles lying around. Thought you might be interested," Riley said. His voice was polite, but Brennan could see a look of amused mischief in his eyes.

"I'm glad you did," the old man said. "I don't get many hits with the sign out there. Most of the marbles come from the eBay." He motioned toward the kitchen, and Brennan saw piles of cardboard boxes stacked in one corner.

"All those were marbles?" Tyler asked. His voice was cautious. He seemed to be somewhere between Brennan's apprehension and Riley's enthusiasm.

"Yup. Name's Glen Bates, by the way."

He reached out a wrinkled hand, and Brennan shook it, minding the swollen knuckle joints. Again, he thought of his own grandparents. His grandfather had arthritis and similar swollen joints.

"We're sorry to bother you so late," Brennan said. "It was inconsiderate of us to drop in like this."

"Not at all," Glen said. "I need all the marbles I can get."

"What got you into collecting marbles?" Tyler asked.

At the question, Glen's face shifted, and sadness filled his already red-rimmed, watery eyes. "My wife."

"Oh," Brennan said. "I'm sorry."

Glen shook his head. "I am, too, but she ain't dead yet, if that's what you thought. Near to it, I'm afraid, but she's still hanging on."

"Does she like marbles, then?" Riley asked.

"I don't think she does," Glen said. "Tries to fight me about it sometimes, but it can't be helped." He turned to look at the boys, then leaned in close, whispering. *"She's lost her marbles."*

"So, you're trying to find marbles like she used to have?" Tyler asked. "To make her feel better?"

"Yes!" Glen said, enthusiasm shaking his voice. "You understand?"

"Uh, sure," Tyler said.

Brennan watched the exchange with mounting concern. Something didn't feel right, and he wanted nothing more than to run back to the car and go back to campus. The fuzziness in his brain had vanished. He swallowed hard and found his voice. "We'd better be going, sir. You can keep the marbles, no charge."

"Hey," Riley interrupted.

Brennan shot him a warning glance.

"Nonsense," Glen said. "Come and see." He waved his hand and walked away from them, down the darkened hallway branching off from the living room.

"What the fuck, man," Riley hissed. "You're blowing it."

"We need to go," Brennan said.

"Yeah, I'm with you," Tyler said. "This is weird."

"You coming, boys?" Glen's voice called from the hall.

"Yes sir," Riley shouted, before either of them could stop him, and stomped down the hall after the old man.

"Fuck," Brennan said, then he and Tyler followed.

Glen stood waiting for them at the end of the hall, his hand curled around the doorknob. "She's in here." He pushed the door open and stepped inside. Dingy yellow light filtered into the hall along with an unpleasant smell. All three men's faces twisted as the odor increased. It was the smell of sickness. The sight awaiting them in the small bedroom stopped them in their tracks.

The old woman lay on the bed and stared back at the visitors. Her cheeks were sunken, and her skin was thin and yellowed. Terribly frail arms lay at her side. She couldn't have weighed over eighty pounds. The one detractor from her slight frame—the thing that demanded all their attention—was the swollen bulge of her stomach. It curved away from her midsection into a bloated ball, and for a horrifying second Brennan thought she might be pregnant. She was grotesque and unnatural, yet pitiful at the same time. Her vacant eyes were sorrowful.

"Been a few months now since it happened. She was always a little forgetful, but when she got to where she didn't remember who I was anymore, I knew what was going on. I've never been the smartest guy, but I knew what was wrong with my Elaine. She'd lost her marbles." Glen walked over to the bed and put his hand on the woman's shoulder, stroking her gently. Her head turned to touch, but she did not react otherwise. "It's a terrible thing to be a stranger to the woman you love. I had to do something. I figured if she's lost her marbles, then I need to get them back for her. Not just any marbles would do. Elaine is an old woman now. She would need old marbles to match. I put up that sign and started buying up marbles on the eBay. She didn't like it much at first. Thought I was torturing her and tried to fight me. She understands now, though. Don't you, Elaine?"

Glen picked one marble from his left palm with his thumb and fore-finger, then held it up in front of the woman's face. Her eyes found it, and she raised her head and opened her mouth. The boys watched in disgust, horrified as Glen dropped the marble inside. The woman swallowed, her shoulders rising and falling with the effort, and then relaxed back into the pillow again.

"Good girl," Glen said. He turned back to the boys and continued, not noticing the horror on their faces. "At first the marbles weren't taking. She would, uh, well, *pass them.*" Glen's face flushed, embarrassed to mention pooping and his wife in the same sentence. "But they've stopped coming out now. She's getting her marbles back, and I think any day now, she's gonna remember who I am." Glen smiled at the men with genuine pride. "She's going to be so proud of me for figuring a way to make her better."

The three men stared at the scene in silence. Even Riley had lost his sense of humor, no longer smirking. An awkward silence passed, and tension built. Sensing the urgency to act, Brennan spoke.

"Mr. Bates, I think you ought to get your wife to the hospital. You've been taking real good care of her, but she doesn't look like she's doing well. I think she needs a doctor."

Glen's forehead crinkled, and his eyes narrowed.

"He's right, sir," Tyler said. "I don't think you should give her any more marbles."

Glen studied the men, his expression growing more fierce by the second. At last, he spoke. "I see. No more marbles, you say? Take her to the hospital, you say? Why? So they can tell me she's only got weeks or even days to live? So they can run their tests and scans and charge me more money than I've ever made in my life to prove my Elaine is dying? No, I won't do that." Glen shook his head, then grabbed handfuls of his wispy white hair and pulled. "She just needs her marbles back, is all. You won't stop me from giving them to her. Not you boys, or nobody else!"

Brennan took a step toward the door and tugged at Tyler's shirt sleeve. "We're very sorry to have upset you, Mr. Bates. We'll leave you and the missus alone now, and we hope she gets better real soon."

They moved down the hall and back to the living room, Brennan bringing up the rear. He had pushed Tyler and Riley in front of him as they left the bedroom. Behind him, he heard the shuffle of feet as Glen followed them. Tyler reached for the door, but his hand froze when they all heard a loud click.

"No," Glen said.

The men turned to find Glen holding an old revolver in his shaky hand. The gun was pointed at Brennan, and he could see it was cocked and ready to fire.

"You'll tell someone what I'm doing here, even though it's no one's business but ours. They'll come and take her away from me." Glen's voice broke on the last words and his eyes glistened with tears. "They'll take Elaine away from me faster than death is already trying. I can't let you do that."

"Please, sir," Riley said, speaking for the first time since they'd arrived in the bedroom. "We swear we won't tell anybody. You're just trying to help your wife. We understand. Just let us go."

Without answering, Glen shifted and pulled the trigger. The blast was deafening in the small living room. Brennan felt the wind whip past his face as the bullet went left, then Tyler screamed.

The bullet hit Riley in the forehead, blowing a splatter of blood onto the wall behind him. Riley crumbled, dead before his body hit the ground. Brennan reeled away, dropping onto his bottom and backpedaling away, eyes wide and disbelieving. Tyler had backed up against the wall behind the door, pressing himself into it. Glen adjusted his aim, leveled the revolver at Tyler, and fired again. The bullet hit him in the temple, and his body slid down the wall, leaving a red trail streaking behind it.

Brennan took a split second to register the horror of this reality. His friends were dead, and he would be too in the next few seconds if he didn't do something now. Without another moment of hesitation, he pushed forward into a crouch and threw himself into Glen's midsection. The old man had been in the process of turning the gun toward Brennan, but had only made it halfway before Brennan's shoulder slammed into his stomach. The gun flew from his hand and he collapsed, gasping for breath. Brennan heard ribs shatter as he collided with the man, and despite the surrounding carnage, he felt a stab of guilt for assaulting the old guy. It was self-defense of the purest form, but he couldn't help but feel bad for hurting him—an old guy suffering from mental issues.

Back on his feet, Brennan started for the door, but halted at the sight of his dead friends. Their bodies lay in heaps in front of the door. He'd have to move them if he wanted to open it and get out. He had the time to do it. Glen still lay on the floor gasping and moaning, but Brennan didn't think he had the nerve to touch them. There was surely a back door off of the kitchen. Giving the old man a quick glance, ensuring he would not be getting back up on his own, Brennan stepped past him and rushed toward the doorway by the hall leading toward the back of the house and presumably the kitchen. He stepped into the darkened room, fumbling on the walls on either side of the entry for a light switch, then froze. A soft, desperate voice called from the hallway.

"Help... me...."

Brennan cringed. It wasn't the voice of Glen Bates, and it was not the voice of either of his friends. It was her. He turned back and rushed down the hall. The door to Elaine's room remained open. Brennan stepped inside and found Elaine now sitting up on the bed. She looked around in confusion, but she was more awake and present than she had been before.

"What's happened? I heard gunfire."

"Everything's going to be okay, Mrs. Bates. I'm going to call the police and they'll get you to the hospital."

"The hospital? Yes, I don't feel so well. But I'm not sure why?" Elaine scrunched up her face in concentration, and Brennan's heart broke for the old woman. "Oh yes," she said. "That's right. I lost my marbles." She smiled in satisfaction at remembering, then her expression changed into one of pained discomfort. Her chin quivered and her mouth opened slightly. Her breathing intensified, causing her bulbous stomach to lurch up and down.

Brennan leaned toward her and put a hand on her shoulder. "Are you okay, ma'am?"

In response, she lurched, and her mouth opened wide. Vomit erupted from her mouth and with it came marbles by the dozens. The hot liquid splashed onto Brennan, and he spun away. Even with her loud, choking retches, he could hear the clatter of marbles hitting the ground. Bile rose in his throat and he ran for the door. His sneaker came down on a few of the slime-soaked marbles now rolling across the floor and the next instant he was on his back. His head slammed into the floorboards with a crack, and his vision blurred.

"My marbles!" Elaine cried between gags. "I've lost them again."

Brennan rolled to his side, hands and knees slipping on the bile spreading across the floor. He tried to stand, but his balance betrayed him and dropped back to one knee. He twisted and sat back down, then pushed himself away from her.

Elaine had dropped onto her hands and knees and was scooping marbles into her hands. One by one, she dropped them into her mouth and swallowed. Brennan gagged in revulsion. Between the sight of the woman choking down regurgitated marbles and the stench of sickness thick in the air, his own stomach spasmed and threatened to send several cans' worth of beer onto his lap. The room spun around him. *Concussion.* The word appeared in his mind, and he knew time was running out. He had to get out of the house.

With fierce determination, he braced himself against a small dresser against the wall and pulled himself to his feet. He stood still and closed his eyes, praying for the dizziness to pass long enough to let him walk. After a moment, he stabilized enough to try it, and took cautious steps toward the door, being careful not to slip. When he stepped into the hallway, he had a split second to register the old man propped against the wall, gun in hand.

Brennan didn't hear the blast or feel the bullet tear through his skull. The impact threw him back into the bedroom, where he landed two feet from Elaine. She stared at the dead man beside her, then called out.

"Glen? I think I got all my marbles back."

ZERO TOLERANCE

Peter Janson sank lower into the padded chair, shifting his body to shield his face from anyone passing the waiting area. He alternated between tapping feet and bouncing knees while the steady drone of office noise carried on around him. Some of his passing co-workers ignored him, others eyed him suspiciously, letting their eyes linger. Were they wondering why he was outside the human resources office?

Peter regretted requesting this meeting. His stomach churned. Beads of sweat popped up on his bald head, despite the cool air blowing down from the vent. Part of him wanted to rush out of the office and send an email, excusing himself from the meeting. *It was a misunderstanding. The issue has been resolved independently. There will be no need to involve HR.*

That would work. It wasn't that big of a deal. He was blowing it out of proportion, right? The code of conduct training stated you should always report any inappropriate behavior in the workplace, but did this really warrant that?

He knew it did and hated himself for trying to worm out of it. Still, that didn't stop him from wanting to abort the mission.

"Mr. Janson? I'm ready for you."

Peter twisted in his seat and tried to ignore the rapidly tightening knot in his stomach. Melinda Buchanan, the HR specialist, poked her friendly face through the doorway. Aside from his new hire orientation and a handful of staff meetings, they didn't interact much. Whenever he saw her around the office, she was always modestly dressed and professional.

"Come in and have a seat," she said, motioning him inside.

He shuffled past her and sat. The door clicked shut and Melinda took her place behind the large oak desk. The overhead fluorescent light glared off the polished wood. The only decoration was the small golden name plate on the edge of the desktop and a framed poster behind her that read **People are our most important asset!**

"I appreciate you scheduling time to meet with me, Peter. What's on your mind?" She beamed a smile and stared intently with wide eyes.

"Well, it's probably not a big deal. I'm not someone who *rats out* co-workers."

"Of course not, Peter. I'm sure your concerns are genuine and given in good faith."

Peter sighed. No turning back now. "Last week, I overheard someone making inappropriate comments to a female coworker."

Melinda nodded. The wide smile never left her face. She pulled a notebook and pen from the drawer beside her and wrote a few words at the top of a blank page in an elegant script. "Go on."

"He was making—*advances* toward her. She was clearly not interested and politely declined his offer for a date."

"I see. Do you know the names of the employees involved?"

This was the moment he dreaded most—name-dropping a coworker to HR. *Snitches get stitches,* he thought. "To be honest, I'm pretty uncomfortable reporting this. Will he find out it was me?"

"Of course not, Peter. Anything you tell me is completely confidential and I will never mention your name during a discussion with the involved employees. Retaliation is strictly prohibited."

"Okay, good." The tension in his shoulders eased.

"You're doing the right thing, Peter. By reporting what you heard, you are improving the culture of Lexan Incorporated. This is how we get better. Now tell me the names of the employees, please."

"Danny Portsmouth. The woman was Valerie Kinkaid." The moment the words were off his lips, relief washed over him. The decision to speak up had weighed on him for days, and now that it was done, he could breathe easier.

"I see," Melinda said. "How did Mr. Portsmouth react?"

"Not very well. He made some comments, and when she walked away, he used inappropriate language. I'm sure she heard him."

"What did he say?"

"I'd rather not say it myself."

"Of course, Peter. I'm familiar with the common acronyms, if you would prefer."

Brian sighed. "In that case, he called her an 'effing c-word.'"

Melinda's pen froze on the page, and she looked up, searching his face. Peter let his eyes drop to his shoes.

"Did either of them know you were nearby and able to hear them?"

"I don't think so."

"Very good. Peter, thank you for bringing this to my attention. Harassment of any nature is not something we take lightly. You did the right thing."

Peter nodded. "So, what happens next?"

"I have everything I need from you, and I will discuss the matter with management and the involved employees. Rest assured that proper discipline will be applied." She smiled, stood, and escorted Peter to the door. "Thank you again, and have a great afternoon, Peter."

Peter nodded. "Same to—" The door snapped shut behind him.

He hustled out of the waiting area. He didn't want to risk Danny seeing him on the way out of HR. A minute later, he was back at his desk, trying to put the whole thing behind him. With each passing moment, the tension and nerves faded, replaced with satisfaction with himself. After all, he wasn't the one who had been inappropriate. Danny should know better. This would teach him a lesson, straighten him up. Danny had a young family at home, and that made the incident even more repugnant. This was a learning moment for Danny. Peter liked that idea. He returned to his workload and lost himself in his usual afternoon routine.

"Hey, Peter."

Peter looked up from his computer screen. "Oh, hey, Bill. How's it going?"

"Living the dream." Bill chuckled at his own joke.

Peter humored him and smiled. "Aren't we all?"

"You bet. Hey, listen, are you still interested in making a move to the sales department?"

Peter snapped his head toward Bill, eyes wide with intrigue. After a few years in accounting, he'd wanted to branch out into sales. Number crunching was fine, but it was lonely work. He missed talking to customers.

"Yeah, definitely. Why?"

"There's an opening. Posting just hit the internal board."

"Really? Did someone leave?"

"No, they let one of those guys go."

"Who?"

"Portsmouth. Dude was schmuck anyway. Arrogant little asshole. Good riddance."

Peter's face paled. *They fired him?*

"You should apply for it. I'll put in a good word for you. You're gonna go blind squinting at spreadsheets all day." Bill frowned. "You feeling okay, Peter? Looking a little pale."

"No," Peter said. He sat up straight. "I'm fine, just tired. Stayed up too late watching the game."

"See, this accounting crap is already killing you. Let me know when you apply, and I'll throw my two cents in with the boss."

"Thanks, Bill. I appreciate it."

Bill gave him a fist bump and walked off.

Peter slumped back in his chair. His stomach churned and reflux burned his throat. It had been three days since his meeting with Melinda. He hadn't seen Danny, but that wasn't uncommon. There were a hundred people onsite, and he was tied to his desk most of the day. The satisfaction he'd felt for doing the right thing evaporated. He'd derailed that man's life—his family's lives. For all he knew, Danny was their sole provider.

And Peter got him fired.

But had he? He thought of the horrible things Danny had said, the hurt and fear on Valerie's face. Still, he couldn't shake the guilt.

Before he could change his mind, he stood and marched to the HR office. Melinda's door stood open. Peter knocked lightly.

Melinda looked up from her computer and flashed her usual wide smile. "Peter, it's nice to see you again. What can I do for you?"

"Do you have a few minutes to speak in private?"

"Of course, Peter. Please, come in and close the door."

He pushed the door closed and sat.

"What's on your mind?"

"I just heard Danny Portsmouth was let go. Was he fired because of what I reported?"

"Of course not, Peter. No one thinks you had any malicious intent. Your actions were in good faith and an exemplary demonstration of supporting a safe and inclusive workplace. In fact, your actions have been recorded in your personnel file as a positive review."

Peter sighed. "Does what he did really warrant termination?"

"I understand how you're feeling, Peter. But at Lexan Incorporated, we have a zero tolerance policy for harassment, and he is accountable for his own actions."

"I get that. I just feel terrible. I know he has a family. I feel responsible for their situation."

"That's very admirable of you. His family is taken care of."

Peter perked up. "Oh, really? So, did he get some sort of severance package?"

"I'm afraid I can't disclose details, Peter."

"Of course," Peter said. "Still, that makes me feel a little better."

"Is there anything else?"

"No. Thank you, Melinda. I appreciate the talk." He walked to the door, then paused, his hand resting on the handle. "Actually, one other thing. This may be poor timing, but since there's an opening in the sales department now, I'd like to apply for it."

Melinda stared at him blankly, her smile twitching at the corners.

Peter shifted his weight to the other foot and fidgeted with the door handle. "I've, uh, always wanted to transition to a role with more direct customer interaction."

She held her silence for another awkward moment, then her smile returned to its prior radiance. "You should apply for the vacant position. It's posted internally now, and we'll begin interviews next week."

"Okay, I think I will," Peter said. He pulled the door open quickly, banging it against his shoe. "Sorry to bother you, and thanks again."

"No trouble at all, Peter."

He shuffled out of the office, feeling her stare lingering on him. *Hope I didn't give the wrong impression,* he thought. The last thing he wanted was to capitalize on Danny's firing.

On his way back to his office, he saw Valerie Kinkaid approaching from the other direction. It was the first time he'd seen her since he overheard the harassment she received from Danny. As she passed, she flashed him a brilliant smile and waved. Her face showed no sign of the disgust and hurt he'd glimpsed when Danny had called her that awful name. In fact, she nearly glowed. Valerie was in a safer place because of him. He'd done the right thing. Danny'd made his own bed.

He put the visit with Melinda out of his mind and spent his lunch break applying for the sales position. Opportunities like these didn't come around every day, regardless of the circumstances. Opportunity was knocking, and he would answer.

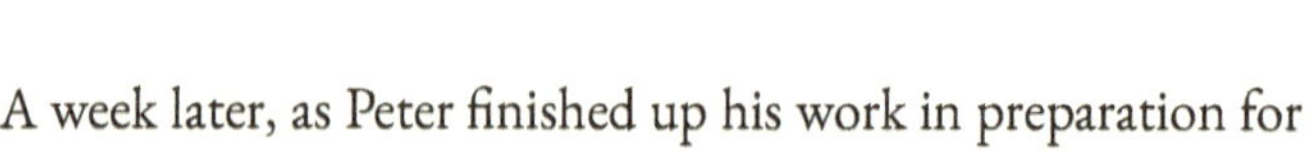

A week later, as Peter finished up his work in preparation for the weekend, an email alert dinged on his computer. It was from Melinda with the subject line **Interview - Sales Representative.** His heart skipped a beat as he clicked. It was also addressed to Robert McKenzie, the VP of Sales.

Good Afternoon, Peter,

We apologize for the short notice, but would you be available at 5:00 PM this afternoon to discuss your application for the vacant sales representative position? The interview will be held in the rear conference room. Please let me know if this will work for you.

Best,

Melinda

"Oh man," Peter whispered. He shot a glance at the corner of the screen. It was already 4:30. This was very short notice. His hands shook as he sent his reply.

Hi Melinda,

5:00 PM works great! I look forward to discussing the position further.

Peter

He jumped out of his chair and made for the restroom. Not much time to prepare. He splashed cold water on his face and checked his teeth. *Good as it's gonna get.*

On his way back to the office, he passed the break room kitchenette. A small crowd was gathered by the water cooler. Snippets of the conversation reached him in the hall as he hurried by.

"So tragic."

"Can't believe he would do that."

"What kind of monster does something like that?"

They must be talking about one of those true crime documentaries or something. No time to stop and ask.

Back in his office, he took a moment to calm his nerves. He scribbled a few notes on the pad by his computer to help focus. **Be confident. Sell yourself. Maintain eye contact. Firm handshake.**

The clock now said 4:45. *It was always good to be early.* He took a deep, steadying breath, then left his office. The rear conference room was deep in the maze of cubicles. As he neared the corner leading away from his hallway, a voice called out from behind.

"Hey Peter, man!"

Peter swiveled. Bill was coming up the hall.

"Did you hear the news? Crazy shit, man. Can't believe he would do it."

"Sorry, Bill. I'm in a rush. I have a meeting I can't miss. Fill me in on Monday, okay?"

Before Bill could reply, Peter was around the corner. He didn't have time for gossip. Most of the offices he passed were empty, the occupants likely ducking out early on a Friday. He rounded one last corner and the conference room came into view. Melinda and a man he'd never met but assumed was Robert the VP waited by the door.

"Peter," Melinda said, "thank you for coming."

"And early to boot," the man said. "I like that. Punctuality is important." The man stuck his hand out as Peter stopped in front of him. "Robert McKenzie, Vice President of Sales."

"Peter Janson. Very nice to meet you, sir."

"Please, come inside and have a seat," Melinda said.

A long rectangular table dominated the conference room. He took a seat midway down one side. Pamela and Robert sat opposite him.

"So, Peter," Robert said. "I've reviewed your application. Four years with the company, a stellar performance record, no disciplinary marks against you. You're doing well in the accounting field. What's got you thinking about a move to sales?"

"Well, sir, I've always had a passion for working with people. I have great communication skills, and I think my understanding of our business model from a financial perspective will really give me an edge in communicating the benefits of working with us to potential clients."

Robert nodded. "I think you might be right. You seem like the kind of guy who really goes after what he wants. That kind of determination is important in sales. Can't just take no for an answer."

"Yes, sir," Peter said. "I like to think of myself as very self-directed and determined."

"It's too bad, though. Filing a false allegation against a coworker to get him fired so you can take his job?" Robert clucked his tongue.

Peter's jaw dropped. "Excuse me?"

"Don't play coy, Peter. I'm privy to your accusations against Mr. Daniel Portsmouth. As his direct supervisor, I was involved in the process of his termination. Then, lo-and-behold, you apply for his position."

"Sir, that's not at all what happened. I swear, it's just a coincidence." Peter looked desperately at Melinda. "You believe me, right? You said it yourself. I did the right thing."

"Peter, much like harassment, we have a zero tolerance policy against slander and professional sabotage. Spreading lies for your own benefit is strictly prohibited." Melinda smiled at him. "Unfortunately, your actions are grounds for termination."

"And after we went to all that trouble, making it look like an accident. Do you have any idea how much something like that costs?" Robert shook his head.

The conference room door burst open and two men in dark suits swept the room. They flanked Peter, jerking him to his feet.

"What is this?" Peter shouted. He tried to push one of the men away, but the other slugged him in the stomach. The wind rushed from Peter's lungs and he dropped to his knees, gasping. There was a ripping sound and a length of duct tape was slapped over his mouth. He reached to pull it away, but the other man delivered a swift kick to his midsection, dropping him face first onto the carpet. His hands were yanked behind his back and zip tied together. The man cinched them roughly, the plastic sinking deep into the tender flesh of his wrists. He moaned, panting in desperation through his nose. They lifted him off the floor and carried him out of the conference room like a misbehaving toddler.

Peter twisted, scanning the now dark hallway for anyone who could help him, but it was empty. How was this happening? How could they believe he lied about Danny just to get his job?. This was madness.

The men carried him down a darkened hallway in an area of the office he'd never seen before. Janitorial supplies lined the walls until the hall reached a dead end. At the far wall, they dropped him.

Peter rolled over and scooted away from them, pressing himself into the corner. Melinda approached and the two men separated to let her through.

"I'm disappointed in you, Peter. Your false allegations put our company in an unfortunate position. Mr. Portsmouth would have grounds to file a wrongful termination suit against us. That would be bad press, and we simply could not allow that. It's a tragedy what happened, his house burning down with his family inside. I hope they didn't suffer too terribly. I'm told there's evidence suggesting he killed them himself, then set fire to their home to destroy the evidence. The police are searching for him now, but I don't think they will find him. No, I find that unlikely." Melinda leaned down and smiled at Peter. "Those deaths are because of your selfish actions, Peter. I hope you are sorry for what you've done.

Unfortunately, this is where your employment ends. On behalf of Lexan Incorporated, we'd like to thank you for your past service, but your continued efforts will not be needed."

One of the men bent and pulled open a trapdoor on the floor. The other grabbed Peter and lifted him into the air. Peter tried to scream against the gag, but it came through as only a muffled howl. Tears streamed from his eyes, and he tried to kick himself free, but the other man caught his legs. Together, they positioned him over the open trapdoor and dropped him into the darkness.

Peter smacked into a wet stone floor. Pain exploded throughout his body. He rolled onto his back and could barely make out the faces of the two men staring down through the opening. One of them reached under the edge of the trapdoor and flipped a switch. A dim light bulb flashed on. Peter's eyes widened in horror and he screamed again.

Dozens of bodies lay scattered around the small room in varying states of decay. All of them wore dress clothes. Peter rolled to his other side, grimacing against what he was sure were broken ribs, and froze as he noticed another body. This one was fresh. Were it not for the eerie stillness of the corpse, he could believe the man was still alive. He had a name for this face. Danny Portsmouth's corpse stared at him with vacant eyes.

Above him, one of the men chuckled, then flipped off the light. The trapdoor lid closed and impenetrable darkness swelled to fill the space.

Peter screamed for a long time.

Eventually, he stopped.

Are you looking for a new start with a company where employees are our number one asset? At Lexan Incorporated, the sky's the limit for career growth. Join our team of dedicated professionals and reach your full potential.

Now hiring for the following positions:

Accounting Specialist - Full benefit package paid for by Lexan Inc. Salary negotiable.

Contact Melinda Buchanan for more information!

SCAVENGER HUNT

Dusk was upon them. The flashing lights of the police cruisers scattered around the camp created a dizzying display of reds and blues racing rhythmically through the trees and off the cabins. Leslie O'Connor stood by the mess hall watching the flood of people scrambling around the property. The camp was buzzing with activity. Counselors were being interviewed by police officers, while other officers and EMTs ventured into the trees. The parents had arrived in droves earlier that afternoon. Leslie had been in the main office while Henry Duggan, the camp manager, made the calls. One after another.

Hello, this is Henry Duggan. I'm the manager at Camp Skyview. There is a situation here, and I'm afraid that your child is missing. The police are on site.

From there, the conversations turned to stuttering apologies from Mr. Duggan, and cries of disbelief and outrage erupting from the phone speaker. Leslie watched Mr. Duggan's face crumble into tears after every call.

Seven calls. Seven children gone missing overnight.

Leslie was doing her best to keep everyone hopeful, but it was a lost cause. Many of the parents she tried to console had screamed at her.

"How could you let this happen? Why weren't you watching them?"

Leslie had given them all sympathetic nods. She understood their anger and let them be. They were processing their grief and lashing out. If berating her made them feel better, then Leslie didn't mind.

She left her post by the mess hall and wandered across the large open area between the cabins, looking for anyone she might help. As she passed Butterfly Cabin, she heard a soft whimpering. She followed the sound to the back of the building and found Teresa sitting on the ground, her knees pulled up against her chest, sobbing. Teresa was one of the head counselors. She'd been at Camp Skyview every year for the last twelve years; six as a camper and six as a counselor. Leslie sat beside her and wrapped her arm around Teresa's shoulder.

"How could this happen?" Teresa asked. "These kids are our responsibility. They depend on us. How could we let this happen?"

"I don't know, but we're going to find them. You'll see."

"Where could they have gone?" A fresh wave of tears crested down Teresa's cheeks and she moaned. "They wouldn't just leave. Especially not Olivia. She would never wander off. Even if the other kids wanted to. She knows the rules. She's been with me for three summers. Olivia is one of my girls." At that, her voice broke, and the sobs returned.

"I know, Teresa. I promise, we're going to find Olivia and all the rest of them. You'll see," Leslie said. She pulled Teresa into a tight hug, then climbed to her feet and left the grieving counselor alone.

She circled around the cabin and back onto the circular path connecting all the cabins. Leslie saw Mr. Duggan pacing around the fire pit, his hands shoved in his pockets. He saw her approaching and crossed the yard.

"Where could they be, Leslie? This is going to ruin us."

Leslie looked questioningly at Mr. Duggan.

"Now, don't give me that look. Finding the kids is number one priority, of course. But after that, no one will send their kids here anymore. Not to Camp Skyview where your kids can go missing. It'll be the end of this camp." He turned and took off back toward the fire pit, mumbling to himself.

Leslie frowned and continued the path away from the trees. She followed the trail to the edge of the main office, then detoured into the grass. She glanced behind her, but no one was nearby. Everyone's focus was on the trees where they hoped desperately for the thickening darkness to give up the missing children unharmed. Up ahead, the utility shed came into view. It was located approximately fifty yards behind the ring of cabins, nestled up against the edge of the forest.

The hinges squeaked loudly as she pulled the door open, but the sound dissipated into the choir of woodland noises. She pulled the door closed behind her, taking one more look outside to ensure she was unobserved.

Various sporting and swimming equipment lay scattered around the small shed. She stepped lightly across the room, dodging a kickball and a tangled volleyball net. Near the back wall, she squatted down and pulled back a dirty floor mat, revealing a trapdoor with a large metal ring in the center. To her knowledge, almost no one knew about the cellar underneath the utility shed.

Leslie pulled back the trapdoor, revealing a crude wooden ladder. A faint yellow light illuminated the dirt floor. Carefully, she lowered herself down the ladder. The smell of wet earth was overwhelming, but she didn't mind. She lowered herself silently to the floor and turned toward the light.

Seven children sat huddled in the corner. They all whimpered at the sight of her.

"Now, children, why are you upset?"

The children stared back at her with dirty, tear-streaked faces.

"You locked us down here," said a young girl. She lifted her leg, show-ing the metal shackle locked around her ankle. Leslie recognized her as Olivia, the girl Teresa mentioned. "Are you going to hurt us?"

"Of course not. I told you guys we're just playing a game. The biggest game Camp Skyview ever had, and you're all part of it. You kids are the prizes!"

"What kind of game?" Olivia stared up at her with wide eyes shim-mering with tears.

Leslie smiled brightly at the little girl. "Don't you know, silly? It's a scavenger hunt!"

THE LAST STAND OF WINSTON THOMAS

D irk Lawson burst through the rickety cabin door. Lillian sat near the fireplace and scrambled to her feet, alarmed by the wild, disheveled look on her husband's face.

"What's happened?" she asked, reaching toward him.

Dirk swatted her hands away and quickly closed the door behind him.

Lillian watched nervously as he paced around the small cabin, securing doors and fastening wooden planks over the windows, blocking out the last waning light of dusk.

"Mama?"

Lillian glanced at her daughter. Emma looked terribly frail in the flickering gloom, knees pulled tightly against her chest, her nightgown puddled around her slight frame. Her wide eyes darted back and forth between her mother and father.

"It's all right, Emma," Lillian said. She scooped Emma up off the floor and nudged her toward the back of the cabin. "Run along and check on your grandpa for me, please."

"Yes, mama." Emma scurried away and disappeared into the short hall, branching away to the bedrooms.

Lillian watched her go, then turn back to her husband. "Dirk, what is happening?" Her voice quivered with uncertainty.

Dirk positioned himself at one of the windows and peered through a crack in the side. After a tense moment, his shoulders slumped, and he turned to his wife. He sagged against the window and covered his face with dirty palms.

"Never seen anything like it."

"Talk to me, Dirk."

"We were down in the mine. Jake found a cavern we hadn't seen before. It looked promising. We gathered the men and went to work. Things were going fine until Jake found that damned thing." Dirk let out a moan and leaned his head back against the wood. "Why did you have to touch it, Jake?"

Lillian approached him in dismay. She'd never seen such emotion from her husband. "I don't understand. What did he find?"

Dirk sighed. His eyes were full of despair. "I don't know what it is. We thought it was a worm. Bigger than any worm I'd ever seen before, but what else could it be? He was clearing rocks and found that thing underneath one of them. Gave him a good start, then he called us over to take a look. Big, slimy thing wiggling on the rock. No earthly reason for it to be there. We should've known right then. It wasn't natural.

"Dirk, you're not making sense. How does a worm in the mine make you so upset?"

"Because it wasn't a worm, Lillian. It wasn't any creature God put on this earth. When Jake tried to pick it up, that's when we knew."

"What happened when he picked it up?"

"It wouldn't let go, that's what happened. Damn thing attached itself to him, somehow. Like it was made of glue. Soon as it touched his finger, Jake started screaming and slinging his hand around, trying to shake it off, but it wouldn't let go. It wrapped itself around his hand like a snake. We tried to help him, but he wouldn't stand still long enough for us to do anything. To tell you the truth, we were all afraid to touch it, anyway. Then, don't ask me how because I don't know. It split open the side of his hand. Cut him like a knife." Dirk leaned forward and grabbed Lillian by the shoulders. "It slithered into the wound, Lillian." His bloodshot eyes were wide. "It went *inside* him."

"My lord," Lillian whispered.

"I'll never forget the sound of his screams as long as I live. When that thing got inside him, he screamed like he was on fire. You could see it moving under his skin, running up his arm. One of the men was quick-witted enough to take off his belt and cinch it on Jake's arm at the shoulder before it could go any further. Couple of us picked him up and carried him out of the mine. I threw him over my horse and rode back to town, quick as we could. He was delirious by the time we got him to Doc. His arm was purple by then, but the belt worked. You could see it squirming around his arm, but it couldn't get past the belt."

"Thank God for that," Lillian said. "Did Doc get it out?"

Dirk shook his head. "He got it out, alright. I told Doc what happened as best I could. A few of the other men caught up by then and backed me up. I must have sounded like a madman, but I told it as it happened. We warned him not to touch it. Doc put on some leather gloves and went to work. He could see that thing moving under his skin. He knew we were telling the truth. We had to hold Jake down to keep him still, and Doc cut his arm open. Slit him from the shoulder to the elbow. I don't think I could have done it myself, but Doc reached right in there and grabbed that thing. Jake screamed like nothing I ever heard before and fainted from the pain. Doc got a hold of that beast and pulled it out of Jake's arm."

Lillian's face paled, and she pressed a hand over her mouth.

Dirk saw the change and nodded. "I felt the same way." He sighed and closed his eyes. "I wish that was the end of it."

"Oh, no," Lilly moaned. "What happened?"

"The gloves worked, and Doc was able to hold it without it sticking to him like it did Jake. I swear the cursed thing was bigger than before—fatter and longer. I wanted to put a bullet through it, but Doc was fascinated by it. He held it up in front of his face, looking it over and studying. Damn fool to let it get so close to his skin."

Lillian's eyes widened. "Dirk, no!"

Dirk clenched his jaw and nodded. "It shot out from his hands and latched onto his face. Old Doc screamed, and that was all it needed. It slithered right into his mouth and down his throat. We didn't know what to do. It was quick. Doc was grabbing at his neck and clawing at his chest, but it didn't matter. Poor old feller started bleeding all over—out of his eyes and nose, his skin cracked open everywhere. So much blood."

Dirk pushed himself off the wall and paced in tight circles in front of her. "You gotta believe me when I say there was no other way. Doc looked me square in the eyes and it's what he wanted. You have to believe that, Lily."

"What did you do?" she asked. Her voice was quiet, and in her heart, she already knew the answer.

"I shot him. Put him out of that misery."

"Oh, Dirk. I'm so sorry." She grabbed her husband and wrapped her arms around him. He resisted for a moment, then sagged against her.

"I had to do it," Dirk said, his voice cracking through tears. "He was in pain and there was no saving him. I would've wanted the same."

"You did the right thing," Lillian said. "Is the sheriff after you now? Is that why you closed the windows? Do they think you murdered Doc? The men were there. They would back up your story."

Dirk pushed her away and rushed back to the window. "I wish it was the sheriff. I could handle that. God help me, I don't know how to handle *this.*"

"Dirk, I don't understand. What's after you?"

"Doc."

Lillian stared at her husband in stunned silence.

"Doc is after me. Or the thing that used to be Doc."

"You said you shot him. If he's dead, how is he after you?"

"I wouldn't believe it if I hadn't seen it with my own eyes. We were all standing there, none of us sure what to do after I put Doc down. Jake was bleeding all over the floor from his arm, skin as white as a sheet. He was gonna bleed out if we didn't do something. I ran to him to tighten the belt back on his arm. That's when Doc bucked on the floor. Scared us all to death. He jumped again, flopping like a damn fish. He was dead. I put that bullet right between his eyes, but it didn't stop him. That thing was still alive inside him, pushing him around. I couldn't move fast enough, Lillian." He turned to his wife and stared desperately into her eyes. "I couldn't shoot him again fast enough. I froze."

"Dirk, honey."

"He flopped over onto his stomach and pushed himself up. He stood back up. God help me. Half his head was gone, and he stood up. He turned around and looked at us. Those eyes will haunt me until the day I die—dead eyes. His body moved all over. That thing was everywhere inside him. Doc's skin split in places and you could see the worm twisting inside, filling him up. I couldn't move. I don't know what came over me, but I couldn't move. Those men are dead because I froze."

"It's not your fault, Dirk."

"It is," he shouted. "I could've shot him down again, but I didn't. Their blood is on my hands."

"No it's not."

Lillian and Dirk turned in unison to the deep voice from behind them. The old man standing just beyond the flickering fire light was frail and stooped. He shuffled gingerly into the room and locked eyes with Dirk.

"If putting a bullet in Doc didn't kill this thing, putting another bullet in his body wouldn't have done you no good."

"You believe me, Winston?"

The old man grunted. "I believe you. It's in your voice and your eyes. No lies coming from you."

"Father, you shouldn't be up without your cane," Lillian said. She rushed across the room and looped her arm through his for support.

"I can still get around when I need to, Lily, and right now I need to." He patted her hand, then turned his attention back to Dirk.

"You ever seen anything like it, Winston?"

"No, can't say that I have, nothing like what you been talking, but I have seen things I can't explain. You don't live as long as I have without seeing things like that. Now, you said it was after you? Finish your story."

Dirk nodded and continued. "Like I said, Doc stood up, and then he went after the men. Billy was closest to him and Doc latched on to him like a leech. Billy tried to push him off, but Doc knocked him down and fell on top of him. His mouth opened—wider than it should have, like his jaw was unhinged—and a piece of that worm pushed out and slid into Billy's mouth. Doc bit down and cut it loose. Even after it was separated from the whole, it kept moving like it was alive on its own. And then it went right into Billy, just like Doc. Lenny dove onto Doc's back and pushed him off Billy, but Doc rolled with him and latched onto Lenny. It got him, too. It got them all."

"All except you, Dirk," Winston said. "How'd you get away?"

"I ran," Dirk moaned. Tears flowed down his cheeks, leaving dirt stained streaks trailing into his beard. "I ran like a coward, and I left those men to die."

"Knock that off." Winston stomped a foot and silenced the sobbing man. "I gave you the blessing to marry my only daughter because you're a good man, and I knew you'd take care of my girl. I didn't give my daughter to no coward. You did what you had to do to survive and get back to your family. Those men were dead, and that's a terrible thing, but there ain't no sense in you dying right along with em."

Dirk stared back in shock. Winston was a stern man, but he'd never taken such a tone with him before. The harsh words from his father-in-law struck him like an arrow, and a surge of renewed vigor filled him. "You're right, Winston. I'm sorry."

"Don't be sorry," Winston said. "Be strong. Now, you said Doc was after you. What happened when you got out of there?"

"I made it to my horse. No one was around outside, thank God for that, and I rode for home. I looked back and Doc was outside, coming after me. I bore down and rode as fast as Silver could take us."

"I'd say it would take a man half the hour to walk here from town, longer if he's in poor shape, and from the sound of it, he is."

"About right, I'd say."

"Might have given up once you were out of sight," Winston said. He shuffled across the room and stopped by the boarded window. "Pull this back and let me see."

Dirk gripped the wood panel and slid it from the window. Dusk had fallen, but the sky was clear and the early stars provided a soft glow over the prairie. Dirk leaned in beside Winston, and the two men scanned the horizon.

"Dear God," Dirk moaned.

"Yup, I see him," Winston said. "He's coming, alright."

Dirk's horse, Silver, noticed the approaching figure as well and bucked against the leather strap tying him to the post outside. The horse snorted and huffed, nearly frantic as it tried to break free.

Dirk dashed across the room, snatched up the rifle hanging on the wall, and threw open the door.

"Dirk, no!" Lillian screamed.

Winston grunted and shuffled toward the back of the cabin. "Lily, get yourself and Emma ready to move."

Lily froze by the window, torn by indecision between listening to her father and watching her husband.

"Now!" Winston shouted.

Outside, Silver neighed and snorted in protest. Dirk walked past the beast and raised his rifle. The shadowy figure of Doc staggered onward. As it approached, Dirk saw the long tendrils of the creature twisting around him. His hands had split away and wiggling appendages gyrated from the stumps. His skull had cracked open and a thick mass of the glossy, pale skin jutted through the opening. All that remained of Doc was tattered meat and skin. With the creature twenty yards away, Dirk fired. The shot echoed across the prairie, but missed the mark, sending up a spray of dirt as it hit the ground some ten yards behind the creature.

"Dammit!"

He adjusted his aim and fired again. This time, the bullet smacked into what used to be Doc's shoulder, spinning the walking corpse backward, but it stayed on its feet. It staggered forward, faster than before, as if enraged by the bullet wound.

Dirk moaned in despair and fired again as the creature closed in. The bullet hit home, dead center, knocking the creature flat on its back. Silver stomped and bucked in panic, the wooden post creaking and threatening to break under the vigorous tugs of the strap. Dirk watched in horror as the creature flopped over onto its front and pushed itself upright again. He let the rifle slide through his hands, gripped the barrel, and swung the stock of the gun as hard as he could. His aim was true, and the gun hit the creature's head with a sickening crunch, shattering the remaining skull. Brain matter and viscera sprayed the ground as the creature collapsed.

"Stand back," Winston shouted.

Dirk spun to see the old man standing at the cabin door with an oil lamp in his hand. He stepped forward and tossed the lamp in a looping arch at the creature. The lamp burst as it hit the dirt just to the left of the creature. Flames erupted as the spreading oil caught fire. The fire singed the piece of the creature exposed through the top of the mangled skull and it thrashed away from the heat. The creature rolled quickly away from the flames toward Dirk.

"Curses," Winston shouted. "Dirk, you take my daughter and grand-daughter out of here. You ride Silver and get as far from here as you can. I'll take care of this thing."

"Winston, you can't," Dirk said.

"Don't argue with me, son. Take my girls and get them somewhere safe."

Lillian stepped out of the cabin with Emma at her side, a blanket wrapped around her. She started to protest, then her eyes fell on the creature and she let out a blood-curdling scream.

"NOW!" Winston shouted.

The creature stood again and reached for Dirk. He swung the rifle once more, again knocking it into the dirt. He locked eyes with Winston. An understanding passed between them, and Dirk nodded.

"Come on girls," Dirk said. He whipped the leather strap loose from the post, freeing Silver. The horse jerked away from the quivering mass on the ground near them and Dirk barely held on. He climbed onto the saddle, then motioned for Lillian. She rushed forward and pushed Emma up onto his lap, then took his hand and pulled herself onto the saddle behind him. Dirk kicked his heels and Silver sprang forward and away from the cabin.

"What about grandpa?" Emma shouted over the pounding hooves.

Dirk gritted his teeth. He didn't know what to say to his daughter. Lillian buried her face in his back and sobbed.

Winston watched them go for a split second, not daring to let the creature out of his sight for too long. It twisted in the dirt and pushed itself upright again. When it rose, it turned toward the fading sound of Silver's hooves and staggered after them. Winston seized the brief distraction and hurried back to the cabin. At the door, he turned and shouted at the creature.

"Over here, you ugly son of a bitch."

The thing stopped its pursuit of the horse and turned back to Winston, then jolted toward the cabin, invigorated by the prospect of easier prey. Winston ducked inside the cabin and snatched up the other oil lamp he had left on the ground just inside the doorway. He coaxed the creature into the cabin. Its appendages were growing by the second, the tendrils hanging from the arm stumps now dragging on the ground. No one on God's green earth knew what this thing was, or anything about it, but Winston reckoned it was consuming the old doctor's flesh and blood, taking that sustenance into itself—becoming more.

Winston knew his odds of coming out of this alive were slim, but he had hope nonetheless. He'd seen the way the thing flinched away from the fire, and it confirmed his suspicions. Bullets may knock it down and give a temporary respite, but they wouldn't stop it. No, bullets wouldn't do the trick, but fire might. With the creature now fully inside the cabin's front room and closing in quickly, he swung the oil lamp with all his might at the creature's midsection. Flames erupted as the glass busted and oil splattered the tattered clothing that remained. The oil ignited quickly, and the creature spasmed wildly. It made no sound. The thing clearly had no vocal cords, but its body hissed and sizzled as hungry flames consumed it.

The figure collapsed to its knees and fell forward, sending a flaming appendage into Winston's hip. The blow knocked his legs out from under him, and he fell to the floor next to the beast. An audible crack sounded from his lower half, and a lightning bolt of pain erupted throughout his body. The heat from the flaming creature pressed against him, singing his clothes, and he tried desperately to drag himself away, but the instant his legs moved, he screamed in pain and collapsed onto his back.

The creature rolled, and a charred piece of the thing slapped across his face. He could feel it undulating against his cheek. Pinpricks of pain developed and warm blood seeped from his face. Winston's mind flashed back to Dirk's recounting of the events in the mine—the way the worm had slit open that poor young man's arm and forced itself inside. He knew that was what the thing was trying to do now. Trying to escape the flames and infect a new host full of life-giving fluids, to restore itself.

Winston couldn't let that happen.

With a desperate rage, he grabbed the burning body and forced himself to roll on top of it. He nearly blacked out from the pain, but determination propelled him, and he rolled the creature with him, sending them both into the wall. The flames had begun to die down, but enough remained to catch the curtains hanging on the wall. Winston watched as the curtains lit up. Orange flames crawled up the wall and spread. Soon, the flames licked at the ceiling. He felt his skin burning, but was no longer sure if it was from the fire or the creature seeking refuge inside him. All around, the cabin crackled and popped, smoke filling the air until he saw nothing but swirling shadows against the flickering light.

Two miles away, Dirk sat atop Silver and watched the distant flames leaping into the sky. Lillian had climbed down from the horse and held Emma in her arms while they both wept. Tears stung Dirk's eyes as well, but they were more than sadness. A profound respect filled his heart. His father-in-law had made the ultimate sacrifice to save his family. Dirk vowed that should the time come when he was called to do the same, that he would face it with the same bravery. For as long as he lived, he would honor his memory.

This land would forever be known as the last stand of Winston Thomas.

FINAL PHOTOS

"**G**ather round, children. Gather round!"

The man in the crisp white lab coat stood in the middle of the control room and waved his arms, motioning the group of children to close in. He wore a pleasant smile and had wire-framed glasses perched on his nose. Brian thought he looked exactly like a scientist would look.

"My name is Dr. Praschka, but you can call me Dr. P." He smiled, then leaned in towards the kids and whispered. "Just don't call me Dr. Pepper." He laughed out loud at his own joke, and the kids smiled politely to humor the man.

Billy turned to Jessica and rolled his eyes. She stifled a laugh and returned her attention to the doctor.

"I'm glad you all could come today, because today is a very special day here at Imagistar Labs. You children are going to see something the world has never seen before." He crossed the room and pointed toward a large digital display on the wall. "Can anyone tell me what this is?"

"It's the solar system," said a boy near the front of the group.

"Excellent!"

"We're a junior high science club, not first graders," Brian whispered to Jessica. "We know what the solar system looks like."

Jessica smirked, but said nothing.

The doctor tapped the screen. "Who can tell me the name of this planet?"

Several voices called out "Saturn."

"Jesus," Brian said under his breath. "Did the rings give it away?"

Jessica elbowed him sharply in the ribs. He gave her an annoyed glance. But it was a bluff, and they both knew it. Jessica was his best friend, and she knew him better than anyone. Brian was what the school guidance counselor called "gifted". He was extraordinarily intelligent. His test scores put him in the top one percent in the nation. The school had recommended he skip a grade or two, but his parents had disagreed. They knew he wasn't being challenged intellectually, but he was also an awkward child. A thirteen-year-old in high school classes would draw a lot of attention from his classmates. They weren't so far removed from high school themselves not to remember how cruel kids can be to each other. Rather than expose their son to potential bullying, they opted to leave him at his age-appropriate grade level, but seek additional learning for him outside of school. Brian was happy with their decision. He knew he was an unusual kid, and he didn't want to lose the few friends he had - Jessica most of all. She knew his intelligence led to him acting arrogantly at times, and she was quick to put him back in his place.

"That's right. Saturn is a very interesting planet. And today, you children are going to see the closest photographs of Saturn ever taken! Years ago, Imagistar Labs launched a satellite headed for Saturn. The satellite - I call her Betsy - traveled across the solar system and made it all the way to Saturn, where she's been taking photographs, measurements, and collecting all sorts of useful data. Betsy's flight path was programmed to end at Saturn, where she would burn up in the atmosphere, but not before taking a few final photos and sending them back to Earth." Dr. Praschka turned and motioned toward the large display at the front of the control center, beaming with pride. "That, my young friends, is what is happening today!"

There were murmurs of excitement among the group, but Brian's brow creased and he raised his hand.

"Yes, young man, you have a question?"

"Is the satellite entering the atmosphere today, or are the pictures coming through today? Because those two things can't happen at the same time."

The doctor nodded approvingly, clearly impressed. "How very intelligent you are, young sir. That is correct. Saturn is so far away that it takes days for the photograph data signal to reach Earth. The satellite has already entered the atmosphere, and the photograph signals should be received and translated a few short minutes from now. Very good, young man. Very astute."

Brian gave a tight-lipped smile, pretending the compliment did not flatter him, but Jessica knew better.

"Brown nose," she whispered.

Dr. Praschka checked his watch and his face lit up. "It's almost time, children! Everyone, gather around the monitor. Our data analyst, Meisha, should receive the signal now and send the photos to the display!"

Brian and Jessica shouldered their way to the front of the group. As much as Brian acted disinterested when he was with his classmates, he was genuinely excited about the pending photos. Astronomy fascinated him, and he was already leaning toward pursuing a career as an astrophysicist. He recognized what a unique opportunity this was to be among the first to see the sharpest images of Saturn in history.

The room fell silent as they waited for the first image to appear. Excitement buzzed. Brian looked around and saw gleeful anticipation on the faces of everyone in the room, Dr. Praschka most of all.

The large display flickered and then filled with vivid swirls of red and orange. A chorus of oohs filled the room. Brian's eyes widened, and he stared at the photo in awe. He'd done extensive research on Saturn prior to this field trip and had seen hundreds of photos of the gas giant. This photo blew away anything he'd seen before. The clarity was astounding.

"It's beautiful," Jessica whispered beside him.

"I know," Brian replied.

"Magnificent," Dr. Praschka said. His eyes were glued to the monitor, and he seemed to have forgotten there was anyone else in the room. Brian couldn't blame him, and recognized the shared passion they both felt for the wonders of the universe.

The screen flickered again, and a new image appeared. Similar to the last, though closer to the atmosphere than the previous. The swirling bands were larger, and the edges of the picture had blurred. *Heat from entering the atmosphere,* Brian thought. The satellite is burning up.

The next picture appeared and furthered the effects of the last. Not much else had changed, except the quality was lessening because of the extreme conditions of the atmosphere. Brian suspected there wouldn't be many more pictures left before the satellite disintegrated.

"Look," Jessica whispered.

Brian glanced at her, and she pointed near the top right portion of the display.

"It looks like a face."

Brian frowned. In the swirling red, there was a strange shape resembling a face. Two dark spots were framed inside faint lines. It was an illusion; he knew. Just like how people see shapes in the clouds, or how conspiracy theorists claim to see statues on the surface of Mars. It was a trick of the eye. Just the brain creating familiar images out of nothing.

"I see it," Brian said, humoring Jessica.

The next picture in the series appeared, and Brian's eyebrow cocked. The face was more defined in this one, with additional lines and creases in the mix of gasses. *Once you've seen it, you can't unsee it,* Brian thought.

"Whoa," Jessica said. "That's weird."

"It's just a trick of the eye," Brian said, though the longer he stared at the strange face, the more uneasy he felt.

The next picture sent a jolt through him. The darkened spots that had given the shape of the eyes had changed. Bright white orbs filled the center of each.

"That is bizarre," Dr. Praschka murmured. "It must be some sort of reaction between the gasses in the atmosphere. Perhaps resulting from contact with the satellite?"

"I don't like this, Brian," Jessica whispered.

Brian turned and found Jessica staring at him with wide, nervous eyes.

"It's okay," he said, then slipped his hand over hers. A strange feeling rippled through him, and he blushed. Her hand felt good in his. She squeezed it back and turned her eyes back to the screen.

Another picture changed, and there were several gasps. A dark oval had appeared below the glowing white orbs. Even more startling, the red mist around the face had changed as well. Dark crimson lines contoured what incredulously appeared to be an arm.

"Everyone, settle down," Dr. Praschka said. "There's nothing to be alarmed about."

Brian stared at the doctor, and confusion on his face did not match his words. He looked very much alarmed.

The screen flashed to the next picture, and silence engulfed the room. The arm was now reaching toward the satellite. A great hand with long, thin fingers filled the center of the image.

The next picture was obscured, only revealing half of the screen. Something blocked the rest of it. *Not something,* Brian thought. *It's blocked by the fingers holding the satellite.* The satellite image was cocked to a different angle, showing the edges of the mysterious face almost upside-down.

"This is impossible," Dr. Praschka whispered.

Brian winced as Jessica's nails dug into the palm of his hand. He squeezed her hand gently and turned. Her eyes were on the screen, her pale face a mask of horror and disbelief.

The screen flashed once more. The room erupted into shouting. Brian suppressed a moan in his throat and pulled Jessica toward him. She said nothing, but buried her face in his shoulder.

The satellite camera was now directly in front of the face. The glowing eyes shined, reflecting the satellite itself. The face was terrible. Brian thought of nightmares he had had as a child. His grandmother had insisted he accompany her to church when he was seven years old. Brian had never appreciated the message of faith as intended, for he could not stop thinking about the warnings of hell for the non-believers. His young mind, already advanced and immensely creative, conjured up images of the demons who inhabited such a dreadful place. He'd given himself nightmares for weeks until his parents finally informed his grandmother that he should stop attending. What he saw on the screen was like the demons he had imagined, only worse. So much worse. What scared him more than anything was the look of interest on the face. Awareness. Intelligence. Understanding. *You can't tell if something is intelligent from a picture,* he told himself, though he knew it was a lie.

The next picture appeared on the screen and brought about a new silence. The atmosphere of Saturn had grown smaller and the edges of the picture were once again filled with the blackness of space.

"Impossible," Dr. Praschka whispered.

Even more impossible, the hand still held the satellite. The face was barely visible on the right edge of the picture, as if the thing was floating into space while carrying the satellite with it. The next picture appeared and showed more of the same progression; Saturn shrinking into the background while the red fingers and terrible face were still visible.

"It knows," Brian said, unaware he was going to say it out loud until the words had come out. He turned to the doctor, who stared back at him with dismayed confusion. "It knows where the satellite came from."

"How?"

"I don't know. But it knows, and it's coming."

Dr. Prashka paled and shook his head. "That can't be. This can't be possible."

Brian said nothing and turned back to the screen as the next picture flashed. Saturn was now fully visible in the background and streaks of light marked the edges.

"Doctor, I'm getting corrupted data from the satellite," Meisha said.

Brian turned to look at the data analyst, having forgotten her completely. The woman flicked her eyes back and forth between the screen and Dr. Praschka. Her face was drawn tight with confusion and frustration.

"What do you mean, corrupted?" Dr. Praschka asked, unable to peel his gaze away from the screen.

"I'm getting readings from the satellite showing speeds that are, well, impossible."

"It's not impossible," Brian said softly. Meisha turned to look at him, and he was relieved to see there was no hint of disregarding him with being a child. She looked genuinely distraught and eager for anyone's input. "Improbable, yes, but clearly not impossible. Look at the last few pictures. The time between them is getting shorter. And look at Saturn in the background. It's moving away from the planet at an incredible rate. Your data is not corrupted. In fact, if the satellite hasn't been destroyed by the friction at that speed, I think you'll find pictures coming even faster."

Meisha stared at Brian, mouth agape, processing what he was saying. Her eyes were wide and unblinking.

"Process the next picture, Meisha," the doctor said. "Leave it on auto-refresh."

Without a word, she turned back to her monitor and tapped a few keys. The screen flashed and photos scrolled through at a furious rate. They could barely process what they were seeing as the screen flashes increased until the lights in the room throbbed like a strobe light.

As Brian watched the screen with horrified fascination, desperate sobs distracted him. Jessica was still clinging to him, but now her body lurched with each cry. He wrapped both arms around her and hugged her tight.

"I'm afraid," she said, gasping for air.

"Me too," Brian said.

Then, the snapshots slowed, allowing more than a split section to register the blurred photos. At last, a photo remained on the screen. In the foreground, a wispy red digit curled around the lens, blocking the lower portion of the photo. Above that, surrounded by the black space, was an object instantly recognizable.

A blue globe covered in swirls of white clouds.

Earth.

Dr. Praschka stared at the screen in dazed wonder. His mouth moved as if he were trying to speak, but no sound came out.

An alarm sounded on the control board, and Meisha slowly pressed a button, silencing the noise. "The satellite signal has ceased. This is the final photo."

Outside the room, Brian heard muffled shouts and the sound of people rushing down the hall. With Jessica still wrapped in his arms, he steered them through the control room and into the hall. Scattered bits of conversation floated over the rustle of movement.

What the hell is it?

Is it an asteroid?

We're not due for an eclipse, are we?

Brian led Jessica with him down the hall, following the crowds. They passed through multiple corridors and into the lobby. A long panel of glass doors lined the far wall, and he saw a crowd of people outside, staring up at the sky.

The door slid open as they approached and warm spring air greeted them. They walked outside, and Brian turned his face to the heavens.

The sky was on fire; red, orange, and gold. It was like looking at the sun. Except, this time, the sun looked back. Brian's eyes locked onto the glowing white orbs in the sky. The sky met his gaze, and an understanding passed between them.

Brian squeezed Jessica tight and buried his face in her hair.

"Keep your eyes closed, and don't let go," he whispered. "It will be over soon."

THE CEMETERY MILE

Phyllis Fairmont sucked in a lung full of spring air and smiled. The songs of chirping birds engulfed her, and the smell of fresh cut grass drifted on the air. She bent forward and tightened the laces on her worn out Nikes. She was due for a new pair and made a mental note to look the next time she went to the mall. She stretched her hamstrings for a moment, started the timer on her watch, and began her walk.

She had her route memorized—one trip around the perimeter, then follow each path to the end, making a symmetrical lattice pattern, ending back at the entrance for an exact one-mile walk.

The cemetery mile.

She wished she had her headphones so she could listen to an audiobook while she walked, but she'd left the darn things home again. The bird songs would have to do.

Rounding the first corner gave her a sweeping view of the cemetery. The entire thing was flat as a pancake, which didn't bother her. She knew walking on inclines was better for you, but it was hard on her knees. A quick scan of the landscape revealed no one else walking the paths. It was a little unusual, but it was still early.

Sure enough, as she reached the end of the straightaway running the east edge, she spotted another woman just arriving through the rear entrance. The woman saw Phyllis and waved. Phyllis squinted back. Her eyesight was getting worse by the day. The woman stood waiting by the entrance.

"It's me, you blind old bat!" shouted the woman.

Phyllis chuckled, recognizing the voice immediately. "Sticks and stones will break my bones, Connie."

"Yeah, they will because you'll never see them coming!"

Both women laughed. Connie matched Phyllis's pace and followed beside her.

"How've you been?" Connie asked.

"Oh, same as usual, I suppose. Just getting some exercise in before Harold comes home from work."

"How is Harold?"

"Same cranky old man he always is," Phyllis answered.

Connie watched Phyllis while they walked with a hint of concern on her face.

"Everything okay between you two?"

"Oh, we get along fine," Phyllis said. Her forehead crinkled. "Why do you ask?"

"Oh, you know, it just seems like things have been off between you two lately. You haven't mentioned going out and doing anything."

"We're simple folk, Connie. Not a lot to talk about, really."

Connie fell silent for a moment, considering her next words. "Hey Phyllis, when's the last time you saw Harold?"

Phyllis turned to Connie. "This morning. What are you getting at?" Her cheeks flushed red.

"Did he say anything to you?"

"So what if he didn't?" Phyllis stopped in her tracks. "Maybe he hasn't spoken to me in a long time. Is that what you want to hear?" Her eyes filled with tears and her nose glowed red.

"I'm sorry," Connie said gently. "I didn't mean to upset you. I just think it's time you accept what's going on."

"Well, I don't think it's any of your business," Phyllis said. She turned and walked away, picking up her pace.

"Come on, Phyllis. Don't be that way. I'm just trying to help."

"You're doing a piss-poor job of it," Phyllis called back over her shoulder.

"Hey, ladies."

Both women turned and saw a man in dirty overalls coming up behind them. He smiled and waved as he approached.

"Nice weather today, huh?"

"It is nice," Connie said. "How you doing, Merle?"

"Living the dream, as they say," Merle replied, then laughed at his own joke. "Phyllis, how's that old man of yours?"

"Harold is fine, we are fine, and I'd like both of you to stay out of my business and leave me be."

The grin disappeared from Merle's face, and he started after her with Connie in tow. "Well, now, hold on a minute there. I didn't mean nothing by it. I just haven't seen the old coot in a while. Kind of wondering if you've seen him?"

Phyllis turned around and stomped the ground, her face livid with anger. "Of course I've seen him. I see him every day."

"Does he see you?" Merle asked.

Phyllis bit down on her lip, rage boiling inside her. What right did Connie and Merle have to question her about Harold and stick their noses where they didn't belong?

"Does he acknowledge you at all?" Merle asked. His rugged features were soft and concerned behind the dark stubble cloaking his face.

"I'm done with this conversation. Don't you have grass to mow or something, Merle?"

"Be reasonable," Connie said. She reached out to put a comforting hand on Phyllis's shoulder, but she jerked away. "We only want to help you. Harold is gone. He's not with you anymore."

"We may have our problems, but he is still very much with me, and he will be there when I get home. Now, if you'll excuse me. I'd like to go."

Phyllis turned again and walked as quickly as she could manage, but Connie and Merle trotted along behind her.

"You'll feel much better if you just accept it, Phyllis." Merle said.

"It's true," Connie said. "You can't fight it forever, honey."

"Leave me alone," Phyllis shouted, and she started to run. Her chest and lungs burned intensely. She hadn't managed more than a slow jog in years, but she pushed herself harder. She heard faint slaps on the pavement behind her as Connie and Merle followed, but the sound faded a little more with each stride.

As she closed the distance between her and the cemetery gate, she saw a young girl sitting cross-legged a few stones off the path. The girl held a flower in her hand, plucking the petals and watching them float to the ground. Phyllis slowed and studied her. She wore a white bonnet and a pink dress that swallowed her legs. Phyllis had never seen the girl before, and was quite sure she would have noticed such a dated outfit. Kids these days all wore shredded jeans or leggings. The girl turned and smiled at Phyllis as she approached.

"Whatcha running from?" the girl asked. Her voice was light and musical.

"Oh, I'm just running for exercise. Where did you come from? I've never seen you before."

"Maybe you should've looked harder. If you look harder, you might understand things better."

Phyllis frowned. She didn't care for the girl's tone. "You ought to show a little more respect to your elders, young lady."

The girl giggled, and her eyes turned cold. "You ought to show a little more respect to the dead."

Phyllis shivered and her stomach twisted. The girl's words echoed in her mind. Only then did it dawn on her how impossibly pale the girl looked. Hey eyes drifted to the stone next to the girl. The name etched in the weathered granite, barely legible, was Abigail Johnson. Underneath the name, an inscription read **Here Lies Our Beloved Daughter.** Phyllis stared at the dates with growing horror. **Born March 11, 1881 - Died January 25, 1889.**

"Run along, Phyllis. Run home to that empty house," the girl said. She sneered at Phyllis. "Maybe I'll see you there."

Phyllis moaned. The sound of footsteps grew louder behind her, and she saw Connie and Merle approaching. She pushed herself forward and ran away. She heard the girl giggle again, a menacing sound like daggers in her ears.

As she ran toward the gate, several more people appeared, gathering in the rows. Some of them she recognized, but others were total strangers. Some stared at her with sympathetic eyes. Others glared at her with contempt and hostility.

"He's gone, Phyllis."

"You have to move on."

"You'll feel so much better."

"He's not waiting for you, Phyllis."

"How long can you deny it?"

The voices assaulted her from all directions. She gasped and moaned in torment, but kept her eyes forward and focused on the gate, now agonizingly close.

The voices behind her joined in a chorus.

"Open your eyes, Phyllis. He's gone. It's all gone. Everything is gone."

She screamed in defiance and crossed under the tall iron gate of the cemetery. The voices silenced, and she didn't dare look back.

Connie and Merle stopped at the edge of the gate and watched her go, then fade from sight.

"Maybe next time," Merle said, his voice dripping with sadness.

"I hope so. I can't stand to watch her go through this," Connie said.

"The funny thing is, she walks right by the stone every morning, but she won't see."

Connie nodded agreement. "Maybe next time."

They turned and followed the path back into the cemetery. Merle faded and disappeared after a moment, but Connie walked a little further. She stopped at a stone midway down one of the aisles. It was a beautiful dual stone with angels carved into the top. Fairmont was engraved in large letters across the back. She stared sadly at the names on the front.

Harold Fairmont

Born 17 July 1957

Died

Phyllis Fairmont

Born 2 December 1959

Died 22 October 2019

"Maybe next time," Connie whispered, fading away into the sun.

THE WEDDING GIFT

V ince held the cabin door with one hand while his other held the train of Lisa's dress up off the ground. The wooden slats of the front porch were thick with damp leaves and moss, and he hated the idea of staining her beautiful dress.

Lisa smiled warmly at him as she passed the threshold. "Thank you, husband."

Vince smiled back. *Husband.* He loved how the word rolled off her tongue.

"I wish I could carry you inside, you know, the proper way."

"If you carry me inside, we'll be spending our honeymoon in an emergency room," Lisa said. "Besides, I need you to save your back for tonight." She gave him a mischievous grin and winked.

His heart fluttered at the thought of the night's festivities, and he tried to fight off the wave of shame he felt over his inadequacies. A car accident a year prior had left him with a fractured vertebra. Physical therapy helped, but he still hadn't reached a point where lifting something over twenty pounds didn't send his lower back into excruciating pain. Lisa did everything she could to assure him it didn't bother her, but Vince couldn't help but feel ashamed at times, like watching her load a case of water into the cart at the grocery store because he couldn't do it.

She must have sensed his discontent because she stopped and wrapped her arms around his neck. "You heard me earlier, right?" she asked. "In sickness and in health. I choose you." She pressed her lips to his, and they kissed passionately.

"Yes ma'am," Vince said when they finally separated. "Make yourself comfortable, and I'll go start a fire."

"Very nice," she said. "I'll go change."

Vince watched her go with a dumbstruck smile on his face. She looked ravishing as she crossed the cabin and disappeared into the bedroom. The wedding was perfect. It was a small, intimate ceremony with their closest family and friends. The weather cooperated, and they gave their vows on the edge of a lake. It was everything he imagined it would be. They would spend their first night as husband and wife at this cabin, then tomorrow they were off to the airport and a five-day stay in Hawaii.

He was still tending to the fire when she emerged from the bedroom. She wore leggings and one of his baggy sweatshirts. "Back to your natural apparel," he teased.

"Hey, I like to be comfortable." She wandered over to a large bay window looking over the lake. The sun had fallen behind the trees, covering the surface with shimmering golds. "It's so beautiful here."

Vince came up behind her, wrapped his arms around her shoulders, and kissed the top of her head. She snuggled up against him and laced her fingers into his.

"It's perfect," he said.

They stood in the window for a moment admiring the scenery, then Vince gave her a light squeeze. "You hungry?"

"I'm still stuffed from dinner."

"How about some wine, then?"

"Hmm, that sounds good."

Vince crossed to the kitchen and pulled out the wine bottle he requested when booking the cabin. He popped the cork and poured them each a glass.

"Come, my dear. Let us sip the finest wine by the fire."

Lisa laughed at his exaggerated accent.

"My goodness, you sure know how to treat a woman."

"Oh, you've no idea."

She joined him, and they sat together on a loveseat facing the fire. The flames had picked up nicely, filling the cabin with warmth and the pleasant smell of burning wood. Lisa draped her legs across Vince's lap, and he massaged her foot. They fell into a silence interrupted only by the soft crackling of the fire. The quiet was nice. As magical as the wedding day had been, it was a relief to be free of the buzz of people. All the planning and hard work prepping for the wedding was done, and now they could enjoy the honeymoon and start their life together.

They finished their glasses, then another. Full dark had fallen, and the cabin was lit only by the flickering glow of the fireplace. Vince moved to get up and fill their glasses once more, but Lisa stopped him. She pushed him back onto the loveseat and climbed on top, straddling his legs. She held his face with both hands, tipped his chin back, and slowly leaned forward. They kissed softly at first, then picked up intensity, tongues flicking and dancing against each other. Vince let his hands slide up her back and underneath the sweatshirt. She moaned, then leaned back, breaking the kiss. She pulled the sweatshirt up over her head, revealing a lacy bra he had never seen her wear before. He breathed heavily as she grabbed his hands and pressed them against her breasts. He grabbed her hips and flipped her sideways onto the loveseat. His back twinged in protest, but the heat of the moment and the alcohol dulled the pain. He hastily unbuttoned his dress shirt, flung it across the room, then lowered himself gently on top of her. Lisa clamped one hand on the back of his head, running her fingers through his hair while they kissed. Vince slid his hand down her stomach and under the edge of her waistband when a sharp crack rattled the window.

"Shit," Lisa shouted.

Vince jerked upright and looked at the window. An ugly crack had appeared, snaking across the center. "What the hell?"

"Somebody's out there," Lisa whispered. She slid off the couch, one hand covering her chest, and snatched the sweatshirt off the floor. She quickly yanked it over her head. "Somebody threw a rock or something."

Vince stared intensely at the spider-web crack. The combination of lustful excitement and adrenaline made him jittery. He crossed the cabin and looked out the window. A crescent moon cast pale light on the lake, but did nothing to penetrate the trees lining the rest of the perimeter. He studied the area for any sign of movement, but saw nothing.

"Do you see anything?" she asked.

"No, but that doesn't just happen. There's got to be someone out there."

"Probably just kids being stupid. I'm gonna call the cabin office, though. I'll be damned if we're going to pay to get that window fixed."

He stomped across the room, irritation swelling within him, and grabbed his phone off the kitchen counter. He scrolled through the list of recent calls, looking for the office number, when Lisa gasped.

"Holy shit," she whispered and jumped to the side of the window, out of view. "There's someone out there. I saw him."

Vince dropped the phone back on the counter and rushed over to the window. "Where?"

Lisa leaned around the edge of the frame and looked. "He was over there by that opening in the trees, to the left of the driveway."

Vince strained his eyes and watched for movement, but everything appeared still.

"I'm not playing around with this shit," he said, then hurried toward the door.

"What are you doing?" Lisa asked, panic rising in her voice.

"I'm taking care of this."

"Vince, no! Don't go out there."

"This is our wedding night, and I'm not letting some dipshit ruin it for us." He pulled open the cabin door and stepped out onto the porch before she could reply.

The temperature had fallen significantly since they arrived, and the cool air reminded him he wasn't wearing a shirt. Lisa stepped out onto the porch and pressed in behind him.

"Hey, you out there? What do you think you're doing?"

He waited, but got no reply other than the sound of crickets chirping.

"I mean it. I'm gonna call the cops if you don't get out of here. This is private property."

Somewhere in the dark came a low chuckle.

Lisa squealed, then clamped a hand over her mouth. Vince's flesh rippled with goosebumps. For the first time, he felt a tinge of fear mixing with the adrenaline surging through him.

"You think this is funny, asshole?"

"Vince, stop. Let's just go inside and call the police."

Again, a soft chuckling sound emanated from somewhere within the trees.

"Last chance. Get out of here or else."

Lisa buried herself in Vince's side, and he wrapped his arm around her. He felt her trembling, and her fear ignited his anger. This was supposed to be a magical night. No one was going to ruin that.

"Alright, asshole. You asked for this. Don't say I didn't warn you."

He peeled himself free of Lisa's grip and stormed down the porch steps. Leaves and twigs crunched and poked at the bottom of his bare feet, but he was running on unfiltered intensity and pressed on. He could hear Lisa calling for him to stop and come back, but she sounded far away, and he kept his eyes on the tree line in front of him. A branch jerked unnaturally, and a dark shape disappeared behind the foliage.

"I see you," Vince shouted.

A crashing sound behind him caused him to spin around in surprise. Lisa lay on the ground in a heap, scrambling to get back to her feet.

"Are you okay?" Vince asked with concern. He tried to help her stand, but she slapped his hands away.

"You idiot! What are you thinking?"

Vince stared back at her in stunned silence.

"You're just going to chase some weird guy into the woods? Don't you watch movies? That's how people end up dead."

"I just—"

"You just what, Vince? Are you trying to get us killed? We need to go back to the cabin and call the police. Now."

Vince considered arguing, but the fierceness in her eyes was foreign to him, and he didn't like it. The adrenaline of the moment was fading, and the uncomfortable reality of their situation dawned on him.

"Okay, you're right. I'm sorry, babe. I lost my head there." He turned back to the woods again, looking for any sign of movement. "Let's go back inside, and we'll call the police. I think I scared him off, but we'll make sure."

"Please," Lisa said. She was still upset, but her anger softened now that Vince was on board with her plan. She let him pull her close, and they started the short walk back to the cabin. The door stood open, firelight flashing on the interior. As they stepped up onto the porch, she looked across the clearing next to their car and froze.

A young girl stood at the edge of the tree line. She wore a plain white nightgown that puddled up around her feet. Her eyes were wide and shiny in the dark, and her pale skin glowed.

"Oh my God, Vince, look."

"What?" Vince turned, then followed her gaze. His fingers clamped down on her shoulder when he saw the girl.

"What the fuck?"

Lisa couldn't take her eyes off the girl, who stared back with a look of infinite sadness.

"Help me." The girl's voice barely carried across the clearing, a delicate tremor in the wind. She turned and disappeared into the trees.

Lisa launched into action and rushed down the small staircase.

"Lisa, wait!" Vince scrambled after her, glancing nervously in the other direction where their first mystery guest had been. "Wait for me!"

Lisa paid him no mind and jogged, then sprinted toward the treeline. "I'm coming, sweetheart," she called out.

Panic filled Vince's mind, and he sprinted after her. In an instant, the canopy of trees blotted out all traces of light, save for the occasional flash of moonlight penetrating the swaying branches.

Lisa slowed her pace, scanning the woods. Vince collided into her back, nearly knocking her to the ground, but Lisa didn't seem to notice.

"Where are you?" she called out.

Vince stiffened at the crunch of approaching footsteps. His upper body broke out in goosebumps, hairs standing on end. Something felt very wrong.

The thing that emerged from the darkness beside them was not human. Though humanoid, its arms were unnaturally long, and it walked on all fours. It reminded Vince of the gorillas he enjoyed watching the last time they'd gone to the zoo. The thing was hairless, lean muscle bulging underneath leathery red skin. A long tail trailed behind it, making a slithering sound as it swept across the leaves and dirt.

Lisa shrieked, and Vince spun her behind him, pushing her away from the monster and urging her to run. The thing snapped its tail like a whip into Vince's lower back. He crumbled immediately; the pain taking his breath away. The sudden collapse dragged Lisa down with him and they lay in a tangle of limbs. Vince wheezed in agony.

"Stay, newlyweds." The creature's voice was soft and disconcerting. "I have no quarrel with you. I've come for the other."

Lisa found her voice. "Not the girl," she said, her voice trembling.

The creature shook its head. "The girl was a trick to draw you out. The man who seeks to invade and destroy, he is the one I will take."

"What man?"

"The man hiding in your cabin."

Lisa and Vince stared at the creature in horror.

"He lured you outside to gain access, and now he waits, as he has done many times before. But no more."

"I don't understand," Lisa said.

"I have spared your lives to rid this world of a pest. Count your blessings and ask me no more questions. His time has come."

"Are you a guardian angel?"

The creature chuckled, revealing a row of razor-sharp teeth.

"If you like. Now, stay."

With that, the creature shot off into the trees, back toward the cabin. Vince and Lisa held each other and waited. A moment later, piercing screams erupted into the night.

STEVE L CLARK

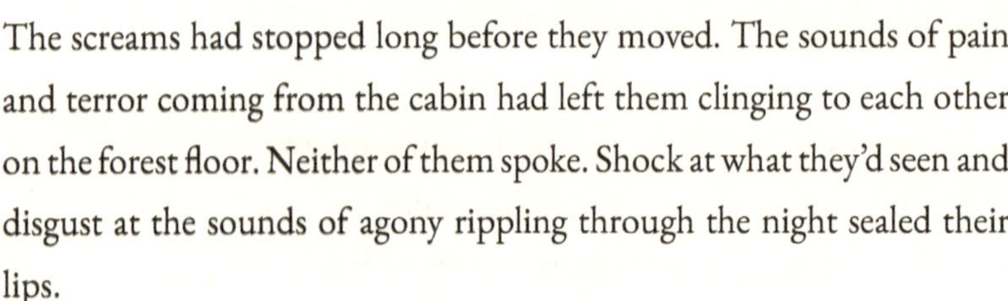

The screams had stopped long before they moved. The sounds of pain and terror coming from the cabin had left them clinging to each other on the forest floor. Neither of them spoke. Shock at what they'd seen and disgust at the sounds of agony rippling through the night sealed their lips.

After nearly an hour of silence, Lisa helped Vince to his feet, and they began the journey back to the cabin. It was slow going. Vince could barely stand. A vicious red welt covered his lower back, and he struggled to stand upright. Lisa helped support his weight, and they took short, measured steps through the trees.

"I don't think I can go in there," Lisa whispered as the treeline cleared, revealing the outline of the cabin in the distance. "It has to be horrible."

Vince grunted. "Our phones are inside. I'll go in and grab one, and we'll call the police." He paused and shook his head. "I don't know how we'll ever explain this. No one will believe us."

Lisa nodded, and her eyes brimmed with tears. "They'll think we did this."

Vince squeezed her hand, but the comfort was hollow. She was right, and he knew it.

The front door of the cabin stood open. The fire had died down to embers, giving the interior a faint orange glow. They stood still and canvassed their surroundings, but nothing moved and all was quiet.

"Okay," Vince said, sliding his arm off of Lisa's shoulder. "Stay here, and I'll go inside and grab a phone." He took slow, cautious steps, careful not to stumble. He focused on the ground, partially to watch for rocks or sticks but also to avoid seeing the carnage inside.

He reached the wooden steps, using the railing as a crutch. At the landing, he took a deep breath, then looked inside. Confusion passed over his face, and he crossed the threshold—the same threshold his wife had crossed while he held her train only hours prior—and flipped the switch beside the door. Fluorescent light filled the cabin, and he gazed in wonder.

"Lisa," he shouted.

"I can't look, Vince. I can't."

To her astonishment, Vince laughed. It was a chuckle at first, gradually building into a fit.

"Come here, babe. You won't believe it."

Timidly, she crossed the drive and climbed the porch steps, wondering nervously if Vince had gone mad from the sight of whatever atrocities had been committed here. Her jaw dropped when he stepped aside and let her in.

The cabin was spotless, save for their belongings. Vince's shirt still lay on the floor where he'd tossed it earlier. Their keys and phones were on the counter next to the wine bottle. All the furniture was as they'd left it.

"I don't understand," Lisa said.

"I do," Vince replied. He put an arm around her waist and pulled her against him. "It means we're going to be okay."

They crossed the cabin, and Vince eased down onto the loveseat. Lisa put a pillow behind his back for support, then paced by the fire in a daze. None of this made sense. She was overcome with a dizzying combination of confusion, terror, and relief.

"I'm cold," Vince said.

Lisa grabbed a blanket from the bedroom and covered him, then picked up one of the neatly stacked logs by the fireplace. She used the poker to bust up the embers, then carefully dropped the log on top. Something on the inside wall of the fireplace caught her attention, and she froze.

"Oh my God," she whispered.

"What is it?" Vince asked. He pushed himself upright, slid down to the floor, and crawled up beside her. She put one hand over her mouth and pointed.

Dark crimson letters were smeared on the wall as if drawn by a fingertip.

You are welcome.

MILES BEFORE WE SLEEP

"**B**abe, wake up."

Brian's eyes fluttered open, and he squinted into the dark. "She's doing it again."

He pushed himself into a sitting position. Lisa lay on her side next to him, already pulling the covers up against her face and closing her eyes. The digital clock on the nightstand was a fluorescent smear. He snatched his glasses from the table, slipped them over his ears, and 2:08 came into focus.

"It's your turn," Lisa said without opening her eyes.

Brian grunted and forced himself out of bed. The wood planks were cold against his soles, but he couldn't see his house shoes in the dark. "I'm going," he mumbled as he navigated around the bed. Closing in on the open bedroom door, he picked up the soft, steady thump of footsteps. He stepped into the hall just in time to see the tail of a nightgown slinking up the attic staircase.

The attic?

Brian huffed and hurried after. "Maria, honey, what are you doing?" He frowned as he passed the open door to her bedroom. Looked like he was going to have to put a lock on it. "Maria?"

He reached the landing. His daughter wandered across the attic toward the single window. It was crescent-shaped and looked out over the backyard. Maria called it her moon view. Once upon a time he was finishing the attic as a playroom or potential guest bedroom. Like most of his *projects,* it remained incomplete, but that didn't stop Maria from claiming the space. She often camped by the window with a book in her hand.

"Maria?"

She pressed her hand against the glass.

Brian waited for her to start up again, but she remained still. He tried to keep his frustration in check. *Never wake a sleepwalker.* That's what they'd been told. Over the last several months, he and Lisa had gotten plenty of practice trying to coerce Maria back to her bedroom. It got easier with time, but also increasingly frustrating. They talked to her pediatrician and were told it wasn't uncommon. Some kids do it, some kids don't. She'll grow out of it.

Brian crossed the attic, careful not to startle her, and put his hands on her shoulders. "Let's go back to bed, honey." He gave her a gentle nudge away from the window. Her fingernails raked the glass as her hand pulled away. Brian winced. The sound set his teeth on edge. Shaking his head, he guided her back down the stairs and to her room. She followed his direction without resistance and climbed back into bed at his urging. He pulled the blankets up to her chin. Her blank eyes stared at him and through him.

"Close your eyes and go to sleep."

Her eyelids snapped shut.

Brian waited. She usually didn't get back up once they got her settled, but something was different this time. He thought of her standing at the crescent window, her little palm pressed against the glass. Each time before, she marched without stopping until they put her back to bed. She'd never stopped before, and something about it bothered him. Perhaps irrationally so.

Satisfied she would stay put, Brian returned to their bedroom. He wanted to tell Lisa about the window, but her soft snores told him to leave her be. Instead, he lay in bed, stared at the ceiling, and listened for Maria until sleep took him.

The following morning, Brian sat at the dining room table watching Maria eat her cereal. Lisa had already left for work, and he would be dropping Maria off at school on his way. He'd chosen not to mention anything to Lisa about the unusual addition to the sleepwalking routine. Something about Maria frozen in place, palm pressed against the glass, felt private, wrong, like something he shouldn't have seen.

As she finished the last few marshmallows floating in her bowl of Lucky Charms, Brian stood and pushed his chair in. "We've got to get moving, kid. You're going to be late."

"I know, I'm going," Maria said. "I'm just tired."

"I bet," Brian said. "Can't get very good sleep when you're walking around the attic."

Maria cocked her head. "Huh?"

"You were sleepwalking again last night."

"I was?"

"Yep. I found you in the attic this time, looking out your moon view."

Maria giggled. "Are you teasing me?"

"Nope. You don't remember that?"

"No." She carried her bowl to the sink and poured out the milk. "I never remember when I sleepwalk." She skipped into the living room. Her backpack hung by the door, and she slipped the straps over her shoulders. "I had a bad dream last night, though. I remember that."

"Oh yeah, what about?" Brian led them outside and locked the door behind them.

"There were people in the sky, and they came to get me."

"People in the sky? That sounds scary."

"It was."

"What did you do?" Brian asked as they climbed into the car and pulled onto the street.

"I ran and got Mommy. You weren't there, though. The people in the sky said they needed her, too."

"What did the people look like?"

"I don't know. I didn't see them. I could just hear them."

"Oh. Well, it was only a dream. Nothing to worry about. Besides, I wouldn't let anybody take you. Not even sky people."

"How would you stop them?" Maria asked. "You can't fly."

"Oh, yes I can."

Maria giggled. "No, you can't."

"Sure can. I have rocket boots in my closet."

She laughed until he pulled up to the school drop off line. She pecked him on the cheek and climbed out. "You should pick me up today in your rocket boots and fly me home."

"Maybe I will," Brian said with a smile. "Have a good day. Maybe you can take a nap when you get home."

The line monitor waved at him as he pulled away, and he watched Maria trot into the school through his rearview mirror. He was relieved she was in good spirits. Fatigue was expected with the increasing sleepwalking occurrences, but her mood and personality were bubbly as ever. *Getting yourself all worked up for nothing,* he thought.

"Nora's daughter is sleepwalking, too."

They were on the couch watching a reality show after putting Maria to bed. Brian looked up from his phone. "Nora?"

"You know, Katie's mom? We were talking in the pickup line at school today. She said Katie's been sleepwalking, too."

"Weird," Brian said.

"Yeah, and do you know what else is weird? I called Dr. Pruitt this morning to ask about it again. Is there anything we can do? She said she's had several parents recently asking about sleepwalking."

Brian stared at her in surprise. "Seriously?"

"Yeah," Lisa said. "How weird is that?"

Brian shook his head.

"Makes you wonder. Is something going on? Something in the water?"

He chuckled, but he didn't actually find it funny.

"I'm serious," Lisa said. "It's weird, and I don't like it."

"Neither do I, but I'm sure it's just coincidence. I used to sleepwalk, too, when I was a kid. She's gonna grow out of it."

"I hope she grows out of it soon," Lisa said. "She's freaking me out."

Brian smiled but said nothing. The commercial break ended, and the show returned, distracting Lisa from the conversation. He didn't want to add to her discomfort, but the truth was, he was equally unsettled. He still hadn't told her about the incident in the attic. Adding those details might push her over the edge.

The show ended, and they trudged to bed, stopping briefly to peek in on Maria. She slept peacefully, and they left her alone. In bed, Lisa curled up beside him, and he ran his fingers lightly through her hair until she slept. He listened for any sign of Maria, but the house remained quiet. Eventually, he closed his eyes and thought about the attic window until he fell asleep.

Brian woke to Lisa climbing out of bed. She crossed the room and vanished into the hallway before he could gather his thoughts enough to speak. *She must be up again,* he thought. He considered following Lisa, but it *was* her turn. He'd wrangled Maria the night before. Plus, Lisa hadn't tried to wake him. So, he dropped his head back on the pillow and closed his eyes. He drifted on the edge of sleep, but also listened for Lisa to return or the sound of the girls passing by on their way back to Maria's room. Neither of those things happened. *How long has it been? Five, ten minutes? What's taking so long?*

No longer able to stifle his concern, Brian stood and stepped into the hall. The attic door stood ajar. It had been closed when they'd gone to bed. His heart rate intensified as he approached the staircase. *What if Lisa tripped on something in the dark and got hurt? What else could they be doing up there?* He rushed up the stairs. At the landing, he froze.

Lisa and Maria stood side by side at the crescent window, each with a single palm placed flat against the glass. Neither moved nor acknowledged his presence. Brian stared in confusion. Seeing his wife mimicking the strange behavior of their daughter unleashed a torrent of uneasiness through his body, and he realized his hands were shaking.

"Babe?" His voice was barely audible. "What are you doing?"

Lisa did not respond.

"Lisa? You're scaring me." His voice trembled.

When she did not reply again, Brian took a timid step forward. The floor creaked under his weight, but both girls were oblivious to the sound. He closed the distance between them and slowly leaned in beside his wife.

Her eyes were wide open, staring out the window. Maria did the same. Neither of them blinked. He followed their stares through the glass. Nothing stirred in the yard or street below.

"Babe," Brian whispered. He gently squeezed Lisa's shoulder. "What is it? What are you looking at?"

Lisa did not respond.

Fear gripped him, and he shook her shoulder. "Lisa, wake up!"

Lisa's free hand flashed upward, striking Brian across the cheek. He stumbled away, clutching his stinging jaw. His eyes watered from both pain and fear. Brian had never seen Lisa show physical aggression toward anyone as long as he'd known her. He'd thought her incapable of violence.

"Lisa, please."

A dull buzzing sound filled the air. At first, he thought one of them was humming, but the sound came from outside, its volume steadily increasing. The hairs on his arm stood as the pressure mounted on his eardrums, and he clamped his hands over his ears. Then a blinding flash of green light erupted outside, filling the attic with an unnatural glow. The buzzing ceased, but the air was alive with energy.

In unison, Lisa and Maria turned toward each other.

"It's time," Lisa said.

Maria nodded.

Their hands dropped from the window, and they turned and marched toward the staircase. They descended, and only when Maria's head disappeared from view did Brian snap to action.

"Girls, wait!" he shouted as he sprinted across the attic. He rushed down the stairs, taking two at a time. He emerged into the hall to find them already at the other end and moving downstairs to the first floor. "Stop! Where are you going?"

He chased after them, adrenaline rushing through his veins. *This has to be a dream.* When he reached the ground floor, Lisa was at the front door, snapping the deadbolt and pulling it open. Maria waited patiently at her side.

Brian sprinted across the foyer and threw himself into the door, slamming it shut. Nothing made any sense, and he couldn't explain it, but his instincts told him if the girls went outside, he'd never get them back.

Lisa turned toward him, brow furrowed. Then she marched toward the kitchen. Maria followed, her face emotionless.

Brian raced around her, stopping in front, and grabbed her hands. "Please, babe, stop this. I need you to stop."

Lisa jerked her hands free, then pushed him away.

"Lisa, please," Brian sobbed. "I don't know what's happening. Please, stop."

Lisa ignored his pleas and continued into the kitchen, Maria trailing behind.

Brian's eyes fell on the back door, and he dashed around the kitchen island to cut her off again. "Stop!" This time, to his surprise, she did. Her head cocked to one side, and she stared at him. "Baby, please. Wake up, okay? I need you to wake up."

Lisa reached to her side and pulled a butcher knife from the block on the island. In one swift motion, she sunk the cold metal into Brian's stomach.

He gasped. Before he could react, she pulled the blade free, then stabbed again. Her eyes never left his as she drove the knife into his midsection again and again. His stomach was on fire. Warm blood streamed down his legs and pooled on the tile floor. Maria stood behind her mother, watching silently.

After a dozen stabs, she stopped. Brian watched in a daze as she slid the red blade back into the knife block, leaving drops of blood on the counter. She turned and walked back to the living room. Maria stepped aside, then followed, not giving her father another look.

Brian stumbled after them. His strength was fading rapidly, and the coppery taste of blood filled his mouth. He coughed a spray of red mist onto the refrigerator as he passed, splattering blood on Maria's school pictures and drawings stuck to the fridge door. In the living room, the front door opened, followed by the squeak of the screen. He crossed the dark room and followed the girls outside.

The sky glowed green to the east. He stumbled and fell forward, grabbing the support beam. His legs buckled, and he slid down the pole, leaving red streaks on the white finish. His wife and daughter marched into the street, joining a parade of people walking away toward the source of the light. As the life faded from his body, he noticed they were all women and children. No men walked among their ranks. He wondered how many fathers lay dying, like him.

With his last bit of energy, he rolled onto his back. The sky was alive with disc shaped crafts, all of them drifting silently to the east. Somewhere in the distance, a man shouted in pain. Brian wanted to do the same, if only to let the man know he was not alone, but his lungs were full of blood and he could barely breathe, let alone shout.

His head rolled to the side, and he saw his family again, blended into the crowd of walkers. Further down the block, one of the craft had landed. It filled the street, dwarfing the surrounding houses. A panel on the lower section opened, extending a ramp to the pavement. Brian watched the walkers funnel into a line as they neared the craft and marched two-by- two up the ramp. The silhouette of his wife and daughter disappeared side by side into the craft. He wanted to get up and go with them, but he couldn't find the strength to stand. And he was so very cold.

Wherever they were going, he hoped he would see them again. With his last breaths, he watched the steady stream of women and children marching down the street. The slap of mostly bare feet on the pavement became a hypnotizing drone, lulling him toward sleep.

He was so tired.

Perhaps he would close his eyes, take a nap, and all this would be over. A terrible dream.

Yes, he thought as he closed his eyes. I'll just sleep, and this will all be over.

I'll just sleep.

ROSES FOR NO REASON

M y wife left me roses today. I find them on the kitchen table when I get home. At one time they had been a deep scarlet red, but are now faded to an almost translucent white. The petals are dry and stiff, curled and collapsing. When I pick up the bouquet, flakes crumble away, leaving a pile of debris behind. Like my wife, the roses have been dead for some time.

I stare at the flowers for a long time. It should frighten me, this gift from the grave. Instead, I feel sadness. Grief overwhelms me. In an instant, I am back at the memorial service, standing by her casket while a line of friends and family pass by. I shake hands, give hugs, and listen to words of comfort, though there is no comfort to be had. My comfort lies in the cold metal box beside me.

The roses shake as I succumb to wracking sobs, sending dust and petals floating to the kitchen tiles. Anyone nearby will surely think I have lost my mind. My breath comes in ragged gasps, but the tears do not let up. I feel as if a dam has broken inside me, and I am powerless to stop the surge crashing through. My hand tenses and squeezes the bundle of roses. There are thorns, and the death of the flower has done little to lessen the sting of their bite. Blood seeps between my clenched fingers and drips onto the floor. One drop lands precisely on one of the fallen petals, and for a moment it looks as it once did—red and full of life.

I know the roses are a message from her. Roses had been our thing. Not a bouquet on Valentine's Day, birthdays, or anniversary. Those were typical reasons. That was the point. We didn't need a reason. Roses for no reason. Those were the best kind. They were a reminder to find happiness in life, no matter the circumstances. To always remember and appreciate one another. With her gone, I had forgotten that. Somehow, she knows I have forgotten.

You often hear people say that should they die young, they would want their spouse to find love again. I know that's what she would want for me, but it's not what I want. The world has lost its color without her—just like these dead roses scattered on the floor.

I could pretend like I don't know why she left these for me. It would be a lie. There is something after this life. Of that, I have no doubt. I don't know what it is, but I know it's there. The moral conundrum I face is, will I find her there if I force my way in? She did not go on her own accord. What will become of me if I cross that line with intention? Is there an actual hell for people who make that choice? I've never believed that, but the cost of being wrong is significant. I could find myself lost to her for all eternity.

As I stare hopelessly at the decayed flora around me, I have an epiphany. This morbid gift can only mean one thing.

She's calling for me. Our souls are so entwined that, even from the grave, she knows my sorrow and can bear it no more than I can. It makes so much sense; a picture snapping into focus. I stand and search. Room by room, I look for more signs. When I find no more roses in the house,

I am not discouraged. This is right. For the first time since I lost her, I have a purpose.

I step out onto the front porch. The fall air wraps cooling hands around me, rejuvenating my soul. My eyes scan across the yard, then stop in the driveway. There, tucked neatly under the windshield wiper blade of my car, is a single rose. Only a few petals remain, the rest blown away by the autumn breeze. I slap my pockets and feel my car key still inside. I jog to the car, leaving the front door of the house open. The things inside are only things, and they no longer matter. I gently remove the rose stem from the wiper blade and hold it up in front of me. The wind takes the remaining petals in a flourish, and I watch them float away.

I lay the stem in the passenger seat and start the car. I do not question which way to go. She has already told me. I will follow the wind.

As houses and familiar landmarks drift by, I keep my eyes peeled for the next rose. I reach an intersection and pause. A moment of uncertainty grips me. A glance in the rear-view mirror confirms no cars behind me, so I close my eyes and take a deep breath. I open my senses and wait for her to point me in the right direction. I jolt forward as the radio blares to life. An acoustic guitar picks through chords and John Denver sings.

Country roads take me home.

A smile spreads across my face. Of course. Where else would she be waiting?

I turn left and sing along. I no longer need directions. I know exactly where I'm going.

Suburban neighborhoods dwindle, and rural fields and forests claim the landscape. I roll down the windows and breathe in the sweet air. The road narrows the further I get from civilization. I need no confirmation about my direction, but I notice a cropping of roses alongside the road every few miles. They stand apart from the rest of the wildflowers because they don't belong to the wild. They belong to me.

Ahead, I see the faded wooden sign next to a gravel pull-off. Some letters are illegible, but I know what the sign says. *Strohman Picnic Area.* It is a place we visited many times. A place of happy memories. I pull the car into the parking lot. The sound of gravel crunching underneath my tires is music to my ears. The smell of someone grilling meat somewhere nearby permeates the air. I climb from the car and let my eyes glide over the surrounding trees. The leaves are changing, but most have not yet fallen to the ground. Everything is so vivid. My senses are firing on all cylinders, more alive than I can ever remember.

I see the opening in the trees near the back of the lot. It's a trail we hiked many times. It weaves a half mile through the trees before reaching the bank of the lake and wrapping back around to the picnic area. I leave the car and hurry toward the trail. Without looking back, I plunge into the shade of the foliage and make my way toward the lake.

I emerge through a dense patch of trees and see the small section of beach. My breath catches in my throat, and my heart leaps when I see the water. Drifting lazily on the surface are hundreds of roses. I think of the times we sat in this very spot, letting the cool water of the lake soak our feet. It is here that I proposed to her. This is the place where we pledged to be together forever. It is only right that this is the place where we reunite.

I feel no fear or doubt. I step into the lake. The water is frigid, but I do not retreat or slow my pace. With each step, it sluices higher, wrapping icy fingers around my knees, then my groin, stomach, chest, and arms until only my head remains above the surface. Damp rose petals stick to my cheeks. I suck in a deep breath and step again. Cold water surges into my ears and the world darkens.

I open my eyes, and I see her. The water is dark, but she shines like the sun. She smiles and beckons me to come. I step toward her. She opens her arms to embrace me. I see my pain on her face; the grief of losing each other. She longs for this as much as I do. My body threatens to float upward, but I do not allow it. I exhale, sending a stream of bubbles rippling to the surface, and immediately my feet sink back to the muddy bottom. With the last of my energy, I swim forward and wrap my arms around her. This is the last sacrifice we must make. My physical self thrashes to reach the surface and breathe. She holds me in her arms and helps me fight. It is uncomfortable, but I am not afraid. We stare into each other's eyes, and my body shuts down. Darkness fills my vision, but only for a moment.

When I can see again, we are together. She smiles and hands me a bouquet of roses. The petals are red and full.

"What are these for?" I ask.

"No reason," she says. "No reason at all."

AFTERWORD

As always, a big thank you to my wife and kids. Your support and enthusiasm for my work means more than you know. Thank you, Matt Wildasin for another fantastic cover. You knocked it out of the park once again. This collection featured multiple editors. Thank you, Brandon Applegate, Tasha Reynolds, and Don Tackett. You all pushed these stories further than I could have on my own. Thank you, Chuck Buda, for all the calls and texts and motivation. You never let me go too far off the tracks, and I'm grateful to have your support.

And, thank you, dear reader, for choosing to spend some of your time reading these stories. It means a great deal to me, and I hope you walk away with a tale or two that sticks in your mind long after you've put the book down.

If you enjoyed this book and want to help support my work, please take a few minutes to rate and/or review it on Amazon or Goodreads.

Until next time!

ABOUT THE AUTHOR

Steve L Clark is a horror and dark fiction writer from Southwest Ohio where he lives with his wife, three children, and one lazy dog. He is the author of the novellas Down Home and The Doors of Chamberlain, as well as the short story collection The Collapse of Ordinary. To follow Steve for updates, news, and links to his work, visit his website at http: //steveclarkbooks.com

www.ingramcontent.com/pod-product-compliance
Lightning Source LLC
Chambersburg PA
CBHW030145010826
48973CB00002B/730